ROPED

Also by Laura Crum

Cutter
Hoofprints
Roughstock

ROPED

LAURA CRUM

ST. MARTIN'S PRESS ❅ NEW YORK

THOMAS DUNNE BOOKS.
An imprint of St. Martin's Press.

ROPED. Copyright © 1998 by Laura Crum. All rights reserved. Printed in the United States of America. No part of this book may be used or reproduced in any manner whatsoever without written permission except in the case of brief quotations embodied in critical articles or reviews. For information, address St. Martin's Press, 175 Fifth Avenue, New York, NY 10010.

Library of Congress Cataloging-in-Publication Data

Crum, Laura.
    Roped / Laura Crum.—1st ed.
        p.   cm.
    ISBN 0-312-19325-4
    1. McCarthy, Gail (Fictitious character)—Fiction. 2. Women veterinarians—California—Santa Cruz—Fiction. 3. Santa Cruz (Calif.)—Fiction. I. Title.
PS3553.R76R6   1998
813'.54—dc21
                                                                98-21149
                                                                CIP

First Edition: September 1998

10   9   8   7   6   5   4   3   2   1

For Andy Snow,
who also remembers the old Brown Ranch.
You in a greenhouse, me on a horse—who would have thought?

Special thanks to Andi Rivers, my sister and friend.

Thanks also to all the people who have been so supportive during the past year: Barclay and Joan Brown, Jane Brown, Wally Evans, Sue Crocker, Brian Peters, Bob Bishop, Dr. William Harmon, Ruth McClendon, Marlies Cocheret, Cathie Jaroz, Paula Rodrigues, Judy Nielsen, Denise Shawlee, Lynne Shawhan, Laurie King, Linda Allen, Lia Matera, Shery Hulse, Betsy Bambauer, Ray Harris and crew, Jack and Deb Hogan, Tom and Jean Lukens (and Andy and Quinn), Jeanette Bothwell, Kendra Hanson, Joanie Gatz (the real life owner of Dragon), Bob, Stephanie, Austin and Bonny Rivers, Justin, Sid, Simone, Mimi and Luke Brown, Lon Brown, Todd Brown, Craig Evans, and all the others, too many to name, who have touched my life and added to this book.

Finally, I would like to thank my family, the Browns, who have been running a family ranch for four generations. Much of what I am I owe to them.

AUTHOR'S NOTE

All the human characters in this book are completely imaginary, and though Santa Cruz County is a real place, the Bennett Ranch and the town of Lone Oak exist only in my mind.

If you would like to find out more about my mystery series, check out my web site at: http://members.cruzio.com/~ABSNOW; or email me at: laurae@cruzio.com

ROPED

ONE

I saw the leg break. I was standing behind the chutes in Glen Bennett's roping arena, watching the teams go, when the sorrel horse stumbled in his second or third stride out of the box and came up with his hind leg swinging loose.

Oh, no. Please, God, no. I prayed the words. Next to me I heard a man say, "Jesus."

The horse was still running, but with his broken leg flopping disjointedly outward with every stride. Incredibly, he kept going, chasing the steer as he had been trained to do, struggling to gallop on three legs.

"Pull up!" Shouts from the crowd.

The blond girl who was riding looked down, aware that something was wrong. Her partner yelled at her to stop, and she checked the horse to a lurching halt, horrified comprehension dawning on her face.

I watched as if turned to stone while she jumped off and saw the leg dangling uselessly. Her partner got off, too, and put a hand on the leg and moved it gently. No doubt about it at all. The leg had snapped above the hock—a compound fracture. Not fixable.

"Gail." Lonny Peterson's voice behind me brought me back to my senses.

"I'll go get my stuff," I told him.

Turning away from the tragedy in the arena, I headed toward Lonny's pickup, where the emergency kit I always carried with me was stashed. It was Saturday, my day off, but since I was a horse vet by trade, I came to ropings and other horsy events prepared.

In the periphery of my vision, I could see a little knot of people gathering around the injured horse. The blond girl who had been riding him was sitting on the ground, sobbing. Poor girl. Poor horse. But there was nothing I could do except put the animal out of his pain with merciful quickness.

Grabbing the emergency kit from the floor of the truck, I hurried back toward the arena. Glen Bennett intercepted me at the gate.

"Can you load that horse up with enough painkillers so we can move him in the stock trailer?" Glen's voice was level, but concern was evident in the lines of strain around his eyes. The roping arena belonged to Glen—his concern was natural. But it was more than self-interest. I'd known Glen since I was fourteen; he loved horses, had owned and raised them all his life.

I could understand why he wanted to move the horse before we put him down. A dead horse in the middle of the arena creates all sorts of problems, aesthetic and practical.

"Let me look at him," I said. "If he isn't in too much distress, sure."

"I'll have Tim get the trailer."

Tim, Glen's son, standing behind us, nodded at the words. If Glen looked concerned, Tim looked predictably relaxed. In his late twenties, with lazy, quiet brown eyes and a loose, casual air, Tim didn't seem to get worked up over anything. Before Glen could say more, Tim ambled away—not fast, but not slowly either—presumably to get the stock trailer.

Gritting my teeth, I approached the horse. He stood on three legs and sweat was beginning to break out on his neck, but he looked more confused than distressed. I filled a syringe with three cc's of rompin and torbugesic and injected it into his jugular vein. In a matter of seconds, his expression calmed.

I turned to Glen, who had followed me. "Where's the owner? I think it's OK to move this horse, but I should talk to her."

Glen gestured toward the parking lot, and I could see the still-sobbing blond girl being led away by an older woman to a waiting pickup. "She's just a kid," he said. "They're neighbors of mine. I told her I'd take care of the horse."

"You can give me permission to put him down, then?"

"I guess I'll have to."

We both knew this was a ticklish subject. Lawsuits could result if the people involved decided that Glen or I had made a wrong decision. Running my hand down the horse's hind leg, I palpated it gently.

"This can't be fixed," I said.

"I know. Go ahead and put him down. I'll take the blame, if there's any to take. Let's just move him out of here first."

Tim had pulled the stock trailer through the arena gate and had driven up next to the horse. Glen and I loaded him as gently as we could. The shot had taken the edge off his pain, and he hobbled gamely in on three legs, willing to do what he was asked, even under these conditions.

"I'll stay in the trailer with him," I told Tim. "Drive real slow."

Tim nodded and got into the cab of the truck without a word. I could hear Glen talking to him in a low voice: "Put him in back of the barn, by the driveway where the tallow truck can get to him; there's a tarp in there by the hay you can cover him with." Then the trailer was moving forward at a crawl and I stood by the horse, steadying his head and talking soothingly to him.

He stood quietly and I stroked his neck, feeling tears rise in my eyes. Damn. I rubbed my hand roughly across my face.

I didn't know this horse. I'd never seen him before, as far as I was aware. A common-enough sorrel, he looked like he had some age on him, and it was clear he had a kind eye and a nice temperament. I blinked more tears out of my eyes and patted him gently.

He was just another good horse. But neither I nor any other horseman can explain the magic of a good horse to those who don't understand them. The wonderful, biddable, docile nature of these swift, powerful, excitable creatures, the magical quality of their longtime partnership with man. I loved this horse— as I loved all good horses. It was a feeling deeper than logic, and it could make my job harder than it needed to be, which it was doing now.

The stock trailer came to a stop. I wiped my eyes hastily, and Tim came around to help me unload the horse. The gelding got out as willingly as he went in, and I loaded the kill shot.

No point in putting it off. Giving the horse a final pat, I told Tim to steady his head while I injected the shot into the jugular vein. The horse went down quickly and easily, and Tim and I jumped away from his falling body as he collapsed onto the ground, his eyes instantly and permanently blank.

I checked his heart with the stethoscope. All quiet. Giving the sorrel shoulder a final pat as I stood up, I met Tim's eyes.

"Too bad," he said. "This was a good old horse. Dad raised him."

Poor Glen. No wonder he had been willing to take responsibility for the horse. Though it was like Glen to do whatever needed doing. It was a measure of how highly I respected the man that I'd been willing to put the horse down without overt permission from his owner, a veterinary no-no. But I was sure Glen Bennett would take care of it, as he'd said he would. It was Glen's way.

"I'll go get the tarp." Tim disappeared into the barn.

I stood there staring down at the horse's body, thinking that this could be Gunner. I'd been planning on competing in the second jackpot of the day. An accident like this one could happen anytime, anywhere. My horse could be lying there dead.

The thought was almost intolerable. Tears rose to my eyes again, and I hastily brushed them away. Shit. It was just too much. Not now. Not today.

I was wiping my nose with the tail of my shirt when Lonny and Glen appeared around the corner of the barn. Damn. I tried to compose my face.

If Lonny noticed my distress, he didn't show it. Glen had eyes only for the horse. Tim reappeared dragging a tarp, and the men covered the carcass. Tim volunteered to call the tallow truck and moved off. Lonny neither met my eyes nor touched me. I stood there, feeling friendless, and hoped I wouldn't burst into outright sobs.

I'm not usually such a big baby. Putting horses down is part of my job. Not the most pleasant part, but an important part. Saving mortally ill or injured horses unnecessary suffering is a good thing to do, and I knew it. It was just that the last month of my life had been more than ordinarily stressful, and I didn't have any reserves of strength left.

Lonny was seeing his wife again. Lonny, my boyfriend of almost four years, had never quite brought himself to divorce his estranged wife, for financial reasons, he said. Sara, the wife in question, had seemed quite content to live with her doctor boyfriend and accept a monthly check from Lonny. Then, two months ago, the doctor had moved out on Sara and my happy life had disintegrated.

Overnight Sara had decided she didn't like living alone; living with Lonny was apparently preferable. She'd begun calling him, inviting him to dinner, making overtures. Some of which Lonny'd accepted. And I was furious.

Call me unreasonable; call me stupid; call me anything you like. I'd never been jealous in my life, and jealousy was chewing a hole in my gut.

Glen straightened and said impartially to Lonny and me,

"He was thirteen years old; I raised him. He was always a good horse. His name was Streak."

Distracted from my problems, I put a hand on Glen's arm. "I'm sorry, Glen."

He shook his head. "It happens. Nothing anyone could do."

Both he and Lonny stared somberly at the covered shape under the tarp, and I knew more or less what they were thinking. The same things I'd been thinking. Requiem for a good horse. An unexpressed hope that their own wouldn't be next.

Two men in their fifties, in many ways very alike, in others very different, Glen and Lonny had known each other virtually all their lives. Both of them had spent most of those lives owning horses and going team roping; both of them, I had reason to know, truly loved their horses. There the resemblance ended.

Glen was movie-star handsome, if you didn't mind an older hero, with square shoulders and a body that remained trim and hard. He had a square jaw to match the shoulders, winter blue eyes, iron gray hair. Above and beyond all that, he had an indefinable charisma, an inner force that attracted women and men, though in different ways. Men followed Glen; women fell in love. I'd idolized him when I was a girl.

Lonny, on the other hand, was big and untidy, with a rough-featured face that most would call homely and a slight roll over his belt. It was the warmth and boyish enthusiasm in his green eyes that made him appealing, that and a certain sense of virile physical power combined with a sharp intelligence.

Damn. Cataloging Lonny's virtues was making me feel even more miserable. Abruptly I turned away from the two men and the dead horse, then turned back and spoke to Lonny. "I'm sorry. I'm backing out of the next pot. You'll have to find another partner."

"But we're entered." Lonny still wouldn't look at me.

"I'm sorry," I said again. "I can't do it. Not now."

"All right. If that's what you want." Lonny's voice reflected no recognizable emotion.

"That's what I want." Almost stumbling in my efforts to hurry away, I walked around the corner of the barn and toward the hitching rail where I had tied Gunner, tears rapidly blurring my vision. I had to get out of here. Find somewhere I could be alone to cry.

Walking up to Gunner, I patted his shoulder, feeling, even in the state I was in, a little glow of comfort and relief at the sight and the feel of him. Gunner, my big stocking-legged bay gelding with his friendly, clownish expression, was a perpetual comfort in hard times. I climbed on him and pointed him up the hill, away from the arena, toward a solitary oak tree I was familiar with. I knew Glen Bennett's ranch well; I'd spent many hours here as a teenager.

Gunner took the trail in a long, swinging walk, and I let out my pent-up breath. Thank God. At the moment, the one thing in the whole world I wanted was a piece of solitude.

Waves of heat seemed to crackle in the yellow grass around me. Though it was only ten in the morning, I was already sweating. Sweat broke out on Gunner's neck, too, as he climbed the hill. Going to be a hot one.

It was May in Central California, a time when we occasionally got heat waves. This one had been on for a week already, with the temperature hitting a hundred every day up in the hills. The grass had gone from green to bleached gold, and ranchers were bemoaning the early end of the feed.

Gunner lengthened his walk as we neared the oak tree, clearly guessing my destination and as eager for the shade as I was. The heat was already oppressive.

We ducked under the canopy of branches and out of the sun's glare with mutual relief, and I turned the horse so we faced back the way we had come. A small breeze swept up the hill and fanned my face, stirring Gunner's mane. Below us was the roping arena and the crowd of ropers, beyond that the little town of Lone Oak, and beyond that a tapestry of rolling, tumbling coastal hills, thick with wild oats, live oak, and greasewood, falling away to the blue curve of Monterey Bay in the distance.

My God, it's beautiful. I forgot what had brought me here; I forgot the urge to cry. Santa Cruz County must be one of the loveliest spots on earth. I was lucky just to be alive and in this place.

Of course, I'm prejudiced. I was born and raised in Santa Cruz County; to me, it's home. Yet one of my wealthy clients, a woman in her seventies who had been a world traveler, had once raised an arm at the view from her place, similar to this one, and told me, "Take a good look. There's nothing like it anywhere. When I was young, the Riviera looked like this, but it's been overrun. This is special."

I believed her, too. The coast of Central California is special, particularly the gentle half-moon of Monterey Bay and the round-shouldered mountains that frame it. The town of Lone Oak is in the hills just south of Santa Cruz and is as picturesque a place as you could imagine.

To speak of the town of Lone Oak is misleading, really. Lone Oak isn't actually a town, it's more of a place, and there are lots of oak trees. What passes for the town is a store/gas station and a bar/restaurant at the junction of two winding country roads that intersect on the spine of the coastal ridge. The lone oak for which it was named is a huge, ancient tree that sits in solitary splendor next to Glen Bennett's roping arena, which is a stone's throw from the bar and the store.

The Bennett ranch surrounds Lone Oak, and the Bennett family owns the town, what there is of it. It's just far enough away from Watsonville to the west and Morgan Hill to the east and the roads are narrow and winding enough that the place is still relatively isolated. Lone Oak is a tiny slice of Santa Cruz County the way it used to be.

Gunner pricked his ears sharply, and I followed his gaze. A

woman was riding up the hill toward us. A blond woman on a bay horse. In a second, I realized who it was. Lisa Bennett, Glen's daughter, my high school friend. A woman I hadn't seen in over fifteen years.

"Shit," I said softly.

Gunner cocked an ear back at me, and I stroked his neck. It wasn't that I didn't want to see Lisa; I didn't want to see anybody. The urge to cry had evaporated, but I still wanted to be alone.

Lisa rode steadily on, coming my way. I had to be her destination; there wasn't anything else up here but trees and rocks. Gunner nickered at her horse, and the bay nickered shrilly back.

Automatically, I sized the horse up as he approached. Solid bay and not too tall, the little gelding had a willowy, deerlike quality to him that was somewhat unusual for a team roping horse. He looked more like a cutting horse. He also had a pretty head, a bold, bright eye, and a graceful, balanced way of moving. Nice horse, I thought.

By now, Lisa was upon us, and I tried to arrange my face in a welcoming smile. "Hi, Lisa, good to see you," I said.

It was a wasted effort. Lisa didn't smile back. Her eyes were hidden by sunglasses, but her mouth and jaw were tense with strain. "Gail, I need help," she said.

TWO

O h, what with?" I stared at Lisa in consternation, aware that my question was hardly graceful, but too nonplussed to care.

Lisa looked different. In a sense this wasn't surprising; if you haven't seen someone in fifteen years, you expect them to look different. But Lisa didn't just look older, more adult. She looked different in some essential way I could never have imagined. She looked as if she'd been rode hard and put away wet, as the ranchers say. She looked older than the thirty-four we both were, she looked deeply tired, and she looked strung tight, as though the slightest extra strain would be too much. She looked the way I felt, I thought suddenly.

She didn't answer my question, just stared at me from behind her sunglasses with unnerving intensity, or so I imagined. I couldn't really see her eyes.

"The horse you just put down," she said finally, "that wasn't an accident."

I stared back at her, thinking that she'd actually gone over the edge. "Lisa," I said slowly, "I saw that horse break his leg. It was an accident. It wasn't anybody's fault."

Impatiently she whipped the sunglasses off her face, looking for a split second a lot more like the Lisa I'd known in high school. "I can prove it," she said.

We stared at each other in the shade of the tree, no doubt both of us evaluating. What she thought of me I can't say. I'd gained a few pounds since high school, but essentially I look the same—tall, dark-haired, wide-shouldered, with strongly marked brows, a large nose. I still wore jeans and my hair in a ponytail. I must have been recognizably the same Gail McCarthy she'd known.

Lisa was still blond, but her hair, once long and straight, was now short and curly; her figure, once curvy, was leaner and harder; and many fine lines rayed out from the corners of her eyes. These changes were minor, though, compared to the change in her expression. Lisa had been one of the friendliest, happiest people I'd ever known. The only word I could find for the present set of her jaw and the walking wounded look in her eyes was embittered.

Rumor had it Lisa had just left her husband, Sonny Santos, an ex–world champion team roper, which would surely account somewhat for the embittered look. But it was still hard for me to believe that pretty, wealthy Lisa Bennett, the most popular girl in my senior class—head cheerleader, honor student, prom queen, you name it—looked so, well, trashed.

I don't know what she read in my face, but after a minute she said in a softer tone, "It's true, Gail. I can prove it. And I really do need help. Will you stay after the roping and have dinner with me, let me tell you about it?"

I was about to open my mouth to say no, that I was having dinner with Lonny, when I suddenly remembered. I wasn't having dinner with Lonny after all. That's what we'd been fighting about on the way to the roping. Lonny was having dinner with Sara. To try and get everything straightened out, he said. Yeah, right.

No doubt sensing my hesitation, Lisa hurried on. "I've got to go back down there. I'm entered in the roping. Please, Gail, say you'll stay. I'll drive you home later, if you need a ride."

"All right."

Before the words were really out of my mouth, Lisa said, "Thank you," wheeled the little bay, and trotted off down the hill. I stayed where I was, wondering what in the hell I'd gotten myself into.

Not an accident? That was ridiculous. I'd seen it happen. What else could it be but an accident? Still, I'd said I'd stay, so I'd stay.

I'd have to tell Lonny, I thought. Automatically my eyes scanned the crowd below me, looking for his familiar form. When I found it, I was sorry. Lonny sat on his horse, Pistol, in the center of a group of men, all of them talking and laughing while they watched the roping. If Lonny was aware that I was sitting up here under this tree, he gave no sign of it. As far as I could tell, he'd forgotten the dead horse and my distress and was having a perfectly nice day. No doubt relieved at the removal of his currently touchy girlfriend.

He had a point, I thought. I knew I was being a pain in the ass. I knew that, logically, it was neither right nor fair to expect him never to speak to Sara again. I understood that he'd spent his whole life acquiring the assets he currently had and that losing them, or even divvying them up, was going to be torture for him. I sympathized. But I had gone ballistic when I found out he'd accepted her invitation to dinner without telling me.

There was probably right and wrong on both sides. There usually is. But it was too late to take back some of the bitter things Lonny and I had said on the way to the roping, and both of us were smarting.

I hadn't refused to rope because I really thought Gunner was likely to break a leg and die. It could happen, but lightning could strike us, too. I hadn't refused just because I was upset at Lonny. It was a combination of all that and the pain I'd felt at putting the sorrel horse down that convinced me I was too stressed out to rope today. Team roping takes guts and quick reflexes; it happens fast and hard. Ropers need to be focused, or they put themselves, their partner, and their horse in danger. And I certainly didn't feel focused at the moment.

I stared down at the pageant below me, seeing it with the eyes of an outsider. The roping arena full of horses and people, the field next to it crowded with trucks and trailers, the little holding pasture beyond dotted with cattle. As I watched, another team rode into the box to make a run. Glen and Lisa.

Glen was on his blue roan stallion, a horse he called Smoke, the current focus of his breeding program. Lisa rode into the heeler's box on the willowy bay horse I'd seen her on earlier, which didn't surprise me. The bay hadn't looked big or thick enough to be a head horse.

Smoke, on the other hand, was big enough to turn any steer in the pen. "A boxcar that can run," Glen had once called him.

I watched Glen back Smoke into the header's box, a familiar sight. I'd spent many happy days in this arena as a high school kid, riding horseback with Lisa, watching Glen rope. When my parents had finally granted me permission to buy a horse of my own, it had been Glen I turned to for help, and when it became apparent that the $500 I'd saved was inadequate to buy a suitable mount, Glen had sold me one of his own horses, one, I later came to understand, who was worth a good deal more than $500. Lad was a gentle, well-broke, dark brown gelding who taught me whatever I know about horses and their ways and who was my friend. When my parents died in my eighteenth year, rendering me instantly alone and poor, Glen had bought Lad back from me and promised to retire him. I'd visited the old horse several times during the long years of college and veterinary school and always found him grazing peacefully in Glen's back pasture. Lad had died at the age of twenty-six, having had as good a life as any horse could ask for.

That was the thing about Glen. There he sat in the header's

box—crisp shirt, pressed jeans, a white straw cowboy hat on his head. In his expensive saddle, on his pretty-headed blue stallion, he looked heroic. And that's just what he'd been to me—a hero.

When I'd taken up team roping several years ago at Lonny's instigation, I'd been delighted to run into Glen again. Unlike so many of my childhood memories, Glen Bennett seemed undiminished. And unlike the small apple farm that had been my family home and was now obliterated by an ugly housing tract, the Bennett Ranch appeared unchanged and secure, safe in Glen's capable hands.

From my spot on the hill I could see Glen's head move up and down slightly as he nodded for the steer. Al Borba, Glen's foreman, flipped the lever that opened the chute gate, and a brown corriente steer burst out, going full tilt. Glen and Lisa thundered after him.

Smoke caught up to the steer easily, and Glen roped the animal around the horns, dallied his rope around the saddle horn, and pulled the steer away. I saw Lisa come in for the heel shot, standing in the stirrups, swinging her rope aggressively. She roped like she meant to catch something. She always had. Even in high school, when Lisa had been a pretty, silky blond that all the boys were in love with, she'd roped as tough as any man in the arena.

The steer took a funny bounce as Lisa threw her rope, and she only caught one hind leg. She shook her head in disgust as she put slack in the rope to let the steer go. Lisa was accustomed to catching two feet. I noticed that her little bay horse worked well for her.

As I watched Lisa and Glen lope down to the stripping chute at the far end of the arena to put the steer away, a strange motion caught my eye. Someone on the sidelines was waving a sign.

For a moment I was confused—unlike fans of baseball and football, spectators at a roping do not wave placards. Or at least they never had, in my experience. The person holding the sign turned slightly, and I could read the message: "I protest cruelty to animals." My God. An animal rights protester.

Two of them, in fact. I could see two sign wavers, a man and a woman, though I couldn't read the second sign. The woman wore a long skirt and the man wore shorts, and they would have stood out in the jeans-clad crowd even without the signs. I noticed everybody was giving them a wide berth.

Another thought struck me. Had these people seen the sorrel horse break his leg? If so, Glen might be in real trouble.

The animal rights movement has been gaining strength and momentum for the last few years. Its devotees protest such things as rodeo events, raising animals for slaughter, and, in some cases, keeping animals in any sort of confinement. It's hard to generalize about the movement, as its members range from those who are offended at cruelty to animals (count me in) to fanatics who don't believe that animals should be kept as pets and appear to think that all creatures should live completely free.

That this is impractical and ridiculous doesn't seem to have occurred to these folks, and many animal rights activists appeared to me to have very little feeling for or understanding of the animals they were ostensibly trying to save. To kill helpless cattle rather than seeing them live in "slavery" (i.e., a fenced pasture) strikes me as craziness, as does turning domestic animals loose to starve on the already overgrazed open range. Not to mention burning down laboratories, including the animals in residence there, because said laboratories do medical tests on animals.

On the other hand, I'm not one to condone putting animals through unnecessary suffering, and I more or less agreed with some of the intelligent animal rights people I knew. The real question is, What is unreasonable and unnecessary? What is cruelty and what isn't? In my opinion, the answer is a little more complicated than many people like to suppose.

I wondered if the man and woman standing by the arena fence with their signs were on the lunatic fringe or if they were sensible, if perhaps misguided. I wondered if they knew anything at all about horses and cattle. If I had to bet, I'd lay odds they didn't.

The next team rode into the box, and I realized with a pang that it was Lonny and Tim Bennett. I couldn't seem to look at Lonny without feeling that pang—a twinge of longing and fear mixed with the sharp bite of anger. Damn him, after all. Why in the world was he doing this to me?

Oblivious to my tangled emotions, Lonny rode Pistol into the heeler's box, ready to make a run. Tim Bennett was heading on a big roan mare, no doubt one of Smoke's offspring. I saw Tim staring down at Al Borba as Al loaded the steer. Tim and Al didn't get along real well. But then, nobody got along with Al Borba. Except Glen.

Tim nodded for the steer, and Al opened the gate; horses and steer came flashing out in the familiar pattern of team roping. From where I sat it looked almost like a ritual, a tribal dance, men and animals interacting in symbolic ways.

Tim turned the steer and Lonny roped two feet cleanly, Pistol performing his part admirably, like the tried and true performer he was. But when Lonny kicked the horse forward to turn the steer loose, Pistol was dead lame.

THREE

Not Pistol. It couldn't be. I felt almost dizzy with fear.

Pistol took another step and I saw that he was able to bear some weight on the injured leg. It wasn't broken. Thank God.

Relief rushed through me like water; my hand shook as I lifted the reins and clucked to send Gunner forward down the hill. Pistol was off in the right front. I thought I could guess what was wrong.

By the time I reached the arena, Lonny'd gotten off Pistol and was feeling the leg carefully. A group of people had gathered around him, including the animal rights protesters. Everybody looked worried and unhappy. Two accidents in one day was unusual and unnerving.

I tied Gunner to the fence and approached the group. Lonny looked up at me and smiled in relief. "Come have a look, Gail."

I bent down and picked up Pistol's right front, palpating the leg carefully and gently from the knee down to the ankle. Nothing obviously wrong that I could feel. Putting the foot down, I told Lonny, "Lead him forward a few steps."

Lonny clucked to Pistol and the horse limped after him. He

was plenty sore, but he could use his right front leg. Given Pistol's history, I was pretty sure I knew what had happened.

"It's his ringbone, I think," I told Lonny. "He must have taken a bad step and tweaked that ankle. We'll have to x-ray him and see if he's got a bone chip in there. Either way, he's done for today. Lead him over to the barn and run some cold water on it. I'll get the vet kit, and we'll give him a shot of bute."

Lonny started to lead Pistol off, and I looked at the group around me, meaning to say something reassuring. Glen and Tim were right at my shoulder; behind them stood the two animal rights protesters, and behind them was Lisa, down on her hands and knees, scrabbling in the dirt of the arena. She was right about where Pistol had pulled up lame.

"Did he step on a rock?" I asked her.

Lisa looked up abruptly from her task. To my amazement, her face seemed distorted with fear, eyes wide and staring, mouth clenched, skin colorless. She didn't answer me, just got quickly to her feet, aware that all of us were watching her.

"They're aren't any rocks in this arena." Tim's lazy drawl.

It was true. Glen had imported truckloads of sand to build the arena; it was beautifully groomed and rock-free.

"I was looking to see if he stumbled in a hole or something." Lisa mumbled this almost to herself, looking at the ground.

"Lisa, I drug this arena not two hours ago. There can't be any holes." Glen's voice. He sounded worried. But, again, I was sure he was right. A sand arena, properly watered and drug as this one had been, was not going to produce an unexpected hole.

"Is he going to be all right?" Lisa again.

"It depends what you mean by all right," I told her. "He has ringbone in that foot, and he's been lame on it off and on for a few years. Not bad lame, like he is now, just a little lame. But the calcification of the joint caused by the ringbone has been getting worse and worse, and I think he may have taken a bad step and possibly caused some of the calcified material to break

20

loose. A bone chip," I added. "I'd guess that's why he went so suddenly and dramatically lame."

"What do you think caused him to take a bad step?" Lisa was off on some track of her own.

"I don't know. Just putting his foot down wrong maybe. Like a person can twist their ankle for no apparent reason."

I could feel the ropers around me nodding; they were all familiar with the way horses could take bad steps and come up lame for no good reason. It was the stuff of everyday life.

"Let's rope!" Al bellowed at us from the chutes.

Lonny and Pistol were over by the barn. I turned to follow them and the group around me started to disperse when we were all frozen in place by the voice of the female protester.

"Surely you're not going to go on with this abuse after you've already crippled two horses?" The question was addressed to Glen, and the woman's voice was loud and belligerent.

Everyone looked at Glen. Face and voice calm, he replied, "It's unfortunate those two horses were hurt, but this is not abuse."

"You should stop this roping right now." The woman had a high-pitched voice; something about her shrill, strident tone was familiar.

I stared, trying to place her. In a second, I had it. My God. Susan Slater. Disbelieving, I looked at Lisa. "It's Susan," I said.

Lisa nodded "uh-huh" and the woman turned toward us at the sound of her name. "Well, Lisa and Gail. If this isn't a class reunion."

Susan Slater had been in Lisa's and my high school class. I might have recognized her earlier if I'd been paying attention; she looked very much as she had when we were all seventeen. Fair Irish skin, a dusting of freckles that matched her long, curly mane of strawberry blond hair, a slim figure shown off now, as then, in a snug tank top and swirling ankle-length skirt. Susan had always been physically attractive enough. It was her ultra-combative personality that was the problem.

21

In high school she had been the one vociferously pushing any cause going, handing out pamphlets to legalize marijuana, demonstrating against police brutality and the fascist state at the slightest provocation. Susan wasn't quiet about her beliefs. She was in your face if you so much as greeted her, pressing her cause in that shrill voice.

She had her devotees, mostly male. The quiet, bespectacled, shorts-and-sandals-wearing man with her looked like a good example of the type. He seemed quite content to let her do all the talking.

"This roping should be stopped," she announced again.

Glen was losing patience. "Lady, what happened to those horses were accidents. Now clear out of here."

I could have told him that was a mistake. Giving Susan an order was like waving a red flag at a bull. She was likely to dig her heels in now.

Susan opened her mouth and was overrun by Lisa: "I think she's right, Dad. I think you should stop the roping."

Dead silence. Susan's mouth stayed open. Everyone stared at Lisa. This was unheard of.

"What are you talking about?" Now Glen sounded angry.

Lisa looked miserable and desperate. "Dad, please. I'll explain later. Really. I mean it."

For a second, father and daughter locked eyes, and my mind jumped back to the plea Lisa had made to me earlier: "The horse you just put down, that wasn't an accident." Could Lisa possibly mean that what had happened to Pistol wasn't an accident either? It seemed unbelievable.

In any case, this wasn't my job. "I need to take care of Pistol," I told Glen and Lisa. "I'll be over at the barn."

I could hear voices raised as I walked away; the clearest one was Tim's: "Jesus, Lisa, will you quit being an idiot?"

Then I was out of earshot and headed for the barn. I'd left the vet kit back there, I remembered, when I put the sorrel horse down. Hardly very responsible of me, but I'd been too stressed out to care. Hopefully no one had swiped it.

Ropers are, by and large, an honest lot. The vet kit was right where I left it. Lonny had Pistol tied to the hitching rail behind the barn and was running cold water on his leg. I filled a syringe with four cc's of phenylbutazone and injected it into the horse's jugular vein.

Pistol stood quietly for this, like the trooper he was. Pistol was fifteen, and between age and the arthritic condition horse-men call ringbone, he was near the end of his working life. The trouble was, Pistol didn't want to retire.

A big, blaze-faced gelding with a flaxen mane and tail, Pis-tol was not only flashy to look at; he was one of the best heel horses in the state of California. He'd been a rope horse all his life, and it was what he knew. Like Rudyard Kipling's famous Maltese Cat, Pistol played for the glory of the game.

On the occasions when his ringbone had been acting up and Lonny'd left him at home, Pistol had stood stubbornly by the gate of his corral, his head stuck between the bars, a pleading look in his eyes. He wasn't lonely; he had Plumber, my other horse, at home with him to keep him company. Pistol wanted to go roping.

But this might be the end for him. Lonny would never put the horse down unless it was absolutely necessary, but Pistol might have to be retired to the pasture, like it or not.

"What's going on over there?" Lonny was watching the little group of people still gathered in the arena.

"They're trying to decide whether to stop the roping," I said. "It's a long story," I added hastily, not feeling up to explaining the whole thing. I wasn't in the mood to have any sort of long conversation with Lonny, at the moment. "Either way," I said, "I'm staying here and having dinner with Lisa. She said she'd take me home."

Lonny made no answer to that. He stared at the cold water he was playing on Pistol's leg as if looking at the offending limb hard enough could make it well. I knew he was desperately trying to avoid a repeat of this morning's argument.

Lonny hated conflict. He had a sunny temper and an optimistic nature—pleasant traits in a man, I had thought initially. I still thought so, but I had come to realize that the downside was that Lonny wouldn't deal with problems. He tried to ignore them out of existence.

As anybody who has ever been involved with such a person knows, this method of avoiding conflict only leads to more trouble in the end. I'm not much of a fighter myself, being inclined to a self-sufficient, autonomous approach to life, but I will take a stand when it seems necessary. As it was becoming now. I was not about to simply let Sara move back in with Lonny without having at least a little discussion about it.

However, this was neither the time nor the place. Lonny was off the hook for the moment. "Go have dinner with Sara," I told him. "Let me know how it goes." It cost me a lot to get those words out in an uninflected tone.

"All right." Lonny's voice was as carefully uninflected as my own. He rubbed Pistol's forehead gently. "What're we going to do about him?"

"Keep him on bute this weekend. Bring him on down to the clinic Monday, and I'll x-ray him and we'll talk about it then. See, he feels better now." I patted the horse's rump.

"Yeah, he does." Lonny agreed.

Putting the bute into Pistol's jugular vein got the painkiller into his system in a matter of seconds. The horse's eye was calm and relaxed, his expression indefinably but plainly different from the stoic look he'd worn a few minutes ago.

That was the thing, I thought suddenly, that you couldn't explain to people like Susan Slater. That you could learn to understand horses, that you could know, much of the time, what they were thinking, what they wanted, what they needed. That until you could do this, you weren't in a position to say what was good for a horse. You had to know horses to love them.

FOUR

Glen canceled the roping. I don't know what Lisa or, for that matter, Susan said to convince him, but he ordered Al to give all the teams their money back and told everybody to go home. It was unprecedented. There would, I knew, be a lot of talk.

Lisa came to collect me as Lonny was loading our horses up. After inquiring about Pistol and finding he was all right for the moment, she herded me into her pickup, apparently anxious to get me alone.

"We have to stop by the big house first and talk to Dad," she said as soon as we were in the cab. "He's pretty upset."

I could imagine.

Lisa drove her truck, a plain white Ford just like Glen's—the Bennetts had never gone in for fancy trucks—up the ranch driveway. I stared out the window at the familiar view.

Hilly pastures rolled away on each side of the board-fenced drive, which was lined with the vivid orange spikes of red-hot poker plants. The hills dropped away from us to the distant farmland of the Pajaro Valley, and beyond that, almost hidden in the heat haze of midday, lay the bay.

We topped a little rise and bumped over a cattle guard. Then it was all green lawns, trees, and flower beds, with the big red brick house set right in the middle.

Lisa parked the truck and we walked into the house through the back door. The front door at Glen's was a massive wooden thing reached by way of a block-long brick walkway, lined with formal flower beds. Very imposing. Maybe that was why it was avoided by just about everybody. Visitors all seemed to walk through the garage and in the back door.

Joyce had always disapproved of this. Joyce was Glen's wife. His second wife, actually. Tom and Lisa's mother had died when Tim was born, and Glen had married Joyce a couple of years later. Tim and Lisa had always called her Joyce, never Mom. Neither of them liked her; Lisa and I had referred to her in our high school years as Lisa's wicked stepmother.

Joyce was watching TV when we walked in. Seeing her there across the room, I thought she looked exactly as she had when I'd last seen her, well over ten years ago. A fit-looking woman wearing tight black jeans and a vivid blouse with a Western print, Joyce had ash blond hair with silvery streaks that had stayed the same color ever since I'd known her. It was a color that suited Joyce.

She gave us a casual glance as we walked into the room, and her eyes met mine. I couldn't tell whether she recognized me or not. Since I had run in and out of her house on a regular basis during my high school years, I would have supposed I might look familiar to her, but if I did she gave no sign.

Glen and Tim were in the kitchen, and Lisa marched firmly in that direction. But curiosity prodded me. I walked slowly across the living room toward Joyce.

It was a long walk. The living room, like the whole house, was huge. Joyce had designed the place, Lisa had once told me. If so, the house sure said some interesting things about Joyce.

The building was laid out on massive, dramatic lines; I doubted whether a hundred people could make the living room seem crowded. There was a brick fireplace that looked big enough to roast an ox, and one whole wall was made up of giant windows that looked out on a wide brick patio backed by a football field of a lawn. The main room contained several couches, a dozen or more chairs, a couple of tables, and a grand piano, but it still looked empty. Maybe it was the height of the cathedral ceiling; I always felt if I yelled it would echo.

I walked across all this space to where Joyce lounged on a flowered couch that clashed quite badly with the loud print of her blouse. She looked up at me with the expression of a sleepy cat. "Hello, Gail," she said.

So she had recognized me. "Hello, Joyce; how are you? It's been a long time."

"Yes, it has. I'm fine. Are you here at the roping?" she asked without much sign of interest.

"Well, sort of. The roping's over. A couple of horses got hurt, and Glen canceled it."

"That's too bad." She barely glanced at me before her gaze returned to the TV.

I stared at her in mild amazement. Even for Joyce, this seemed a bit much. Joyce didn't rope, but at one time, anyway, she'd had a couple of horses she showed in Western pleasure classes. She knew enough about horses and ropings to know that this sort of thing was not par for the course.

Her round blue eyes were locked back on the TV, though, watching what appeared to be some sort of soap opera. Her face, so surprisingly young-looking from a distance, told a different story up close. I could see the thick layer of foundation, the heavy black line around the eyes. I noticed that the hair spray holding the silver ash hair in soft waves had been applied pretty heavily. Joyce, Lisa had once said disparagingly, spent a fortune on clothes, hairdressers, and the like. The money had certainly bought something, I thought; she looked pretty good from across the room.

Seeing that Joyce clearly didn't want to talk to me, I wandered back toward the kitchen, where Lisa appeared to be engaged in a stormy argument with Tim. Before I reached the long bar covered with shiny tile that separated the kitchen from the living room, Lisa burst out of the open archway as if catapulted and grabbed my arm. "Come on; we're out of here. If you want to talk to me come on up to my house," she hurled in Glen's general direction. Then we were out the door.

A blast of hot air enveloped us as we stepped into the garage; I squinted my eyes against the glare of the noon sun on the blacktop driveway. After Glen's cool, dim living room, it felt like walking into an oven.

The heat didn't seem to register on Lisa. She was bristling with fury and strain, and she moved toward her truck with quick, jerky strides, her eyes snapping familiar sparks at me as she said impatiently, "Come on."

I plowed after her, feeling as if I were wading against a tide of heavy, hot mud. Sweat beaded on my forehead.

I'm not used to this kind of weather. Santa Cruz County has a mild climate; what I was used to was cool, foggy summers and sunny, only slightly chilly winters, with the occasional rain to liven things up. This sort of heat was outside my range.

I climbed into Lisa's truck and looked for the air conditioner. No such luck. The truck was a plain Jane, the sort any dirt-poor rancher would drive. No air conditioner.

Lisa was driving up the road past Glen's house, the truck rattling and jouncing in the potholes as soon as we got off Glen's nicely paved driveway.

"Where are you living?" I asked. "Not in Vincente's house?"

"Yep." Lisa's voice was curt.

Vincente was an old man who had spent his life working for Glen. During the years Lisa and I had been friends, Vincente had lived in a little frame house that dated from the ranch's early days—in the late 1800s. Glen and Joyce had bulldozed the main ranch house to build their mansion on its site, but Vincente's house, which was the original foreman's house and sat in a small valley just over the hill, had survived untouched. Probably because Joyce never had to look at it.

In Vincente's case, untouched really meant untouched. The paint had been mostly a memory, the floor dipped in several places, the roof leaked, and the porch had been about to collapse. I couldn't imagine Lisa living there.

"Vincente died a year ago—a heart attack," she said. "When I moved back here I talked Dad into letting me fix the house up. Vincente would never let Dad do a thing while he was alive, wanted everything just as it was." Lisa flashed a sudden, mischievous, watch-me-get-my-way smile, her old smile. "It cost a little bit, but Dad sprung for it. I couldn't live in the big house," she went on grimly. "I've always hated that house."

The emotion in her voice seemed out of proportion to a house, though I didn't like Glen's house either. It was just too big, too opulent-looking. The wall-to-wall carpeting was too deep, and the furniture was too shiny and velvety. It wasn't the kind of house where you could kick off your dirty boots. But I didn't think that was what Lisa meant when she said she hated the house.

We crested the ridge and I saw Vincente's old house down in the valley below us. The house was in a pretty setting under some big cottonwood trees by a creek, but in Vincente's time its picturesque quality had been swallowed up by the crumbling sadness of disrepair. Now a dark brown picket fence adorned with yellow climbing roses framed a square of lawn, and the house itself looked crisp, with a new roof and a solid porch. It had been painted barn red with dark brown trim, and the overall effect was charming—sort of an English cottage with a California ranch twist.

Lisa pulled up to the gate, and we were met by a volley of barks. "Stupid dogs," she said affectionately.

The dogs in question were jumping up and down just inside the fence. They looked like Queensland heelers, and my heart jolted painfully. My old dog, Blue, a Queensland heeler, had died this last winter at the age of fifteen, and I wasn't over it yet.

"Where did you get them?" I asked Lisa.

"Arizona," she said with a smile in her voice. "They take care of me."

I smiled back. "I had one, too," I told her. "I know what you mean."

She opened the gate and they boiled out of it, racing past Lisa to swarm around me, sniffing my pants leg. "They won't bite you," Lisa said over her shoulder. "They like women."

I kept my eye on them, just in case. Queenslands like to nip. These two, one red, one blue, sniffed me carefully but left my ankles alone, otherwise. I eyed the red dog's bulging belly with interest.

Lisa called her dogs from the porch: "Joey, Rita, get over here!"

The dogs reluctantly gave up sniffing me and trotted back to her. I walked after them.

"Is she bred?" I asked.

"Yeah, she is. Joey's the father. Do you want a pup?"

"Maybe." I looked at the dogs some more, considering them as prospective parents for my own next dog. They looked back at me, sharp, pricked ears pointed attentively in my direction. The blue dog had a black mask that covered half his face, giving him an asymmetrical look that was slightly comical. It reminded me of my horse, Gunner, with his one blue eye and one brown one.

The female was a pretty dog, rust red, with a wide forehead and big brown eyes that were rimmed in black, as though she were wearing eye makeup. She glanced at me in that sideways, wary way that Queenslands do, and I thought she looked just like a little fox.

Lisa opened her front door, and the dogs and I followed her into the house. It had changed a lot since I'd seen it last. The pine plank floor was oiled a smooth, golden brown, and there was a braided rug in tones of brown in the center. A wood-stove sat in one corner, and a long burlap-colored couch and a couple of big overstuffed chairs filled the small space. Nothing fancy, but friendly and comfortable.

The dogs lay down on the rug like it was theirs. I walked around them and followed Lisa into the kitchen. It had wall-paper with a light yellow pattern and new oak cabinets. There was a round wooden table with a butcher-block surface. Lisa got two bottles of beer out of the refrigerator and poured them into glasses and set them on the table. "The sun's over the yardarm somewhere," she said.

I laughed. "I guess so. So what's the problem?" I asked as I sat down.

Thus confronted, Lisa looked uncertain. "I don't know how to begin," she said at last. "It sounds so ridiculous. Dad and Tim don't believe me. They think I'm nuts."

"Just tell me the story. Begin at the beginning."

Lisa was staring at the wall behind the table intently. Her blond curls were tumbled, and there were dusty streaks on her neck and shirt. I watched her watch the wall and saw the look of fear creep back into her eyes. She ran her fingers through her curls. "I don't know where the beginning is."

"What are you talking about, Lisa?" I asked her. Patiently, I thought.

"I'm trying," she snapped. "I don't know where to begin. That horse you had to put down, that's part of it."

"What's the rest of it?"

"Lots of things. Most of them little things. Dad's three-year-old colt was poisoned. Someone left the gopher grain where he could reach it through the fence, and it killed him. Then the pasture gate was left open and the cattle got out on the road. Some dummy hit one and is suing Dad." The words were com-ing out of Lisa in a torrent now. "The hitch came off the truck the other day when Dad was hauling Smoke and Chester to a roping. It was on flat ground, luckily, and the trailer just rolled to a stop. We could have lost them, too. And last week," her face seemed to tighten, remembering, "last week he was working on the tractor and Tim was helping him. They worked on it all Tuesday and started again Wednesday morning. Dad got down underneath it; he wanted to figure out why it wouldn't start. He told Tim to press the starter button; Tim did and the damn thing jumped forward. It's just pure luck that the way Dad was lying none of the wheels touched him." Lisa looked at me defensively. "I know you'll think this is stupid. But Dad and Tim both swore they left that tractor in neutral. There's just been too many things. Dad's worried; I know he is."

"All of those things could easily be accidents," I said slowly. "Things like that happen on ranches. You know they do. More ranchers are killed by their tractors than by almost anything else."

"Bulls and stallions do their fair share, too," Lisa agreed. "But I have a feeling about this. Something's wrong. Someone's trying to get at Dad."

"What would be the point?" I asked her. "If someone is really doing this, the question would be why."

"I know. That's what Tim and Dad said. Why would someone do things to make Dad's life miserable? It doesn't make sense. I just have this feeling. I don't like it, Gail." She was quiet a minute. "It scares me," she added at last.

"Why?" I asked.

"I don't know." Lisa sounded completely frustrated. "I just have this sense that someone unreasonable is, well, stalking Dad, and I'm scared of what they might do next." She gave me a sideways look, just like her red dog. "You don't believe me, do you?"

I sighed. "It's not that I don't believe you. It's just that I'm not sure these accidents you're telling me about add up to a stalker."

"Well, one thing I can prove."

"What's that?"

"That horse you had to put down today, the stalker killed him." Lisa stood up out of her chair and fumbled in the back pocket of her jeans.

"What do you mean?" I asked her.

Lisa dug the thing she was looking for out of her pocket and flung it on the table. "Look at that," she said.

FIVE

It was a piece of cardboard, folded up. I picked it up and unfolded it. Some sand fell out on the table. A piece of cardboard about a foot square, that was it.

"I don't get it," I said.

"I found this in the arena," Lisa said. "Right about where Streak stumbled. I found something else, too. A hole. A pretty deep hole. I'm sure somebody dug it."

I poked at the piece of cardboard with my finger. It had been cut on two sides with what might have been scissors. The other two sides were neat and straight, machine-finished. It looked like it might once have been part of a cardboard box.

"Explain, Lisa. What do you think happened?"

"I think someone dug that hole, dug it deep, right down into the clay. The sand layer's only about six inches deep, you know."

I knew. I'd heard Glen talk about how he built the arena often enough. The natural soil here was heavy black clay, what the locals called dobe mud. It had taken many trucks' worth of sand to create a suitable surface to rope on.

"So, anyway," Lisa went on, "here's this hole, about eight inches in diameter, going down into the clay a foot or so. I think once it was dug, the person put this piece of cardboard over the top and then covered it up with sand. No way anyone could spot it. The hole was right in the path of the head horses coming out of the box. It was only a matter of time until one of them stepped in it."

A million objections jumped into my mind. I started with the first one: "How do you know this piece of cardboard and the hole have anything to do with each other?"

"I saw it fly up when Streak stumbled. Like a dirt clod, only it didn't look right."

We both stared at the piece of cardboard. It was dirt-colored, all right. But it was square and would glide rather than hurtle as a dirt clod would if thrown. I could see that Lisa might have spotted it.

Lisa went on. "I'm already paranoid about accidents. I wondered what in the hell it was and went over to pick it up. It seemed strange. Then I was just scuffing around with my boots to see if there was anything that might trip a horse and I felt the ground give under my foot in this one spot. The sand had caved into it some, but the hole was still there. I cleared it out and looked at it."

"Then what did you do?"

"I filled the hole up with sand and stomped it down so it was solid."

"That's it? You didn't tell Glen?"

Lisa shook her head miserably. "No. I didn't know what to do. Dad and Tim are both so upset with me. Tim's pissed off; he says I'm crazy, but Dad is worried, I think. He just doesn't want to believe it's true. I didn't want to tell them. But I was afraid there might be more holes."

"Is that what happened to Pistol?" I was aghast.

"I don't think so. I didn't find a hole, or any cardboard. I think he just took a bad step."

"So that's what you were looking for in the dirt?"

"Uh-huh. And when old Susan Slater started in on stopping the roping, I took my chance and begged Dad to go along with it."

"What'd you tell him?"

"That I was afraid more accidents might happen and I'd explain later. Dad trusts me, you know, at heart. And Susan was getting ready to make a big stink. Said she was going to lie down in the arena and we'd have to rope over her. Dad just gave up. He's pretty unhappy about it, though. Tim went off the deep end."

Lisa got up and picked up her beer. "Come sit out on the porch," she said. "It's cooler out there. This house doesn't have any air-conditioning."

I'd been noticing this. I followed Lisa out the back door, and the dogs came trotting behind us. The back porch was shady, with a view of the cottonwood trees and the creek. A pleasant breeze blew across it. I settled myself into a solid wooden rocker with a sigh of relief.

A big orange cat jumped into my lap. I looked down at him, startled, and the cat looked up at me, his large yellow-green eyes unworried, and gave a small meow. "Pet me," he said clearly.

"Dammit, Zip." Lisa glanced at me apologetically. "Push him out of your lap if you don't want him there. He likes visitors."

"He can stay." I stroked the cat's wide orange-striped forehead. He had a big, heavy head, like an old tom. He sniffed my fingers delicately, then butted his head against my hand and purred.

"Zip?" I queried.

"Zipper. When he was a kitten, he just zipped around everywhere he went, full blast. He's old and fat now."

"He's a tom?"

"No, he's neutered. His dad was a huge old tabby tom I had, and I guess Zip got a lot of his genes."

The big cat rubbed his head on me some more, then nipped my arm lightly. "You do that again, buddy, and you're on the ground," I warned him.

Lisa shook her head. "He likes to bite. He never bites hard, though."

"Great." I ignored the cat and after a minute he settled into my lap purposefully and began purring. I took a sip of beer. The breeze fanned me, flickering green and silver in the cottonwood leaves. I could hear a faint sound of running water from the creek.

"Just what is it you want me to do?" I asked Lisa.

"Find out who's behind all this, I guess."

"Why me?"

"I don't know who else to ask. Dad and Tim won't help, and I'm not getting anywhere. I've been gone a long time—almost ten years. I don't have a lot of friends here anymore."

"How about the cops or a private detective?"

"Dad would kill me. I did suggest it, and he swore if I did anything like that he'd boot me off the ranch. I believe him, too. He said it was one thing for me to be worrying about this foolishness and another thing altogether to make him the laughingstock of the neighborhood."

"Hmm." Glen had a point. People would talk. You couldn't keep anything a secret in a little place like Lone Oak.

"Besides," Lisa went on, "you're a vet and a vet is a doctor, and in the old days people turned to their doctor for advice on everything. Family squabbles, murders, you name it."

"Hmm," I said again. "I hope you don't think this is going to turn into a murder. Because if you do, we should report it to the police right away, no matter what Glen says."

"I don't know what I think." Lisa sounded confused. "I just know I'm afraid."

"All right," I said, "tell me if I've got this right. You think someone is setting up these 'accidents' for the purpose of harassing Glen. Some of them are nuisance things, but some of them are dangerous. And," I went on, "this person doesn't care if other people are injured along the way. Or animals. This person appears willing for Glen's tractor to kill him. Or Tim," I added. "And they couldn't possibly know which horse would step in that hole, who might be injured or killed."

"They knew it would be a head horse," Lisa pointed out. "And Dad heads."

"So do a lot of other people. Anyway, your point is the stalker is setting up all these bizarre, dangerous accidents to get at Glen. So who has a motive to do that?"

"I don't know." But Lisa looked down at her boots as she said it.

"Come on, Lisa; what do you think? I can't help you if you won't tell me what you know."

"I don't know what to think. I keep telling you."

"But something's on your mind. So what is it?"

Lisa scuffed the porch with the toe of her boot. "Susan Slater lives in Lone Oak now. In that house with the tin roof just across from the bar. She moved here right about when I did, six months ago. And that's when the accidents started to happen."

"You don't think Susan did all these things?"

"I told you. I don't know what to think. But Susan's been a royal pain in the ass. She pickets every time we have a roping, and she's always up here complaining about something we're doing. Using hotshots on the cattle or pesticides on the hay field or whatever. It seems like she's up here every day. She could have done it. She lives not a mile from here. And it's the sort of thing she might do."

I thought about it. It seemed bizarre to me. But then, bizarre was a word you might apply to Susan. "It just doesn't seem like enough of a motive," I said.

Lisa was quiet. She stroked the red dog's muzzle, where it lay in her lap.

"Come on, Lisa; give," I said. "What bothering you, really?"

More silence. Lisa finally met my eyes. "I'm afraid it's Sonny."

"Your ex-husband? Sonny Santos?"

"Yeah, him." Lisa's voice was grim.

"Do you want to tell me about it?" This was obviously a tricky subject.

"Well, actually, I never want to think about the son of a bitch again, much less see him or mention his name, but I guess I have to."

"It was a nasty divorce then?"

"As nasty as it gets. The only good part is we were flat broke, so there wasn't anything to split up."

"So what happened?"

"The usual. Did you ever meet Sonny?"

I shook my head no.

"Well, he was and is damn good-looking, and when I met him he was the world's champion team roper, and he was rich and charming and everything a girl could ask for. I fell for him like a ton of bricks. He could have had any little wanna-be barrel racer in the whole country and he picked me. Lucky me.

"Dad never liked him, but I went ahead and married him and we moved to Arizona, where Sonny was going to train rope horses and we were going to be rich and live happily ever after." Lisa was hurrying now, wanting to get the story over with.

"He started running around on me right from day one, almost, and I figured it out pretty quick, but I just kept putting up with it; I don't know why. I'm stubborn. I don't quit easily, and I hate to admit I've made a mistake. I was determined to make a go of it with Sonny. But it just got worse and worse.

"He spent all our money, we were always broke, and he always had a girlfriend. We fought all the time, and pretty soon he started to hit me."

"He hit you?" This was hard to believe. Lisa Bennett had allowed some dumb team roper to hit her?

"I know. How could I have put up with that? I don't know how, but I did. By then I was threatening to leave him if he didn't clean up his act, and Sonny didn't go for that. It was all right for him to run around on me, but it wasn't all right for me to leave him. As far as he was concerned, I was his property; he owned me.

"Finally, I had enough. I left one night when he was off with some seventeen-year-old. Just took the dogs and cat and left. I didn't dare take any of the horses; he would have killed me for that. I drove straight from Arizona to here and told Dad I needed help."

"What happened?" Though I could guess.

"He came after me. Came to get me back. Dad refused to let him see me. I was living in the big house while we remodeled this place. Sonny showed up one night, and Dad ran him off at gunpoint. It was ugly. I heard every word from where I was standing in the garage. Sonny swore he would make Dad pay."

"So you think Sonny's behind all this?"

"I don't know. I'm afraid, though. I've heard Sonny lives around here now. Tim's seen him occasionally."

"Have you?"

Lisa looked at me with bleak, miserable eyes. "No. But I don't leave the ranch much. Lone Oak is as far as I'll go. I'm afraid Sonny will kidnap me, I guess. And now I'm afraid here, too. I'm afraid all the time, Gail."

SIX

I was digesting this when both dogs leaped up from the porch and ran around the house, trailing shrill, excited barks behind them. Lisa got up and followed, yelling, "Joey, Rita, get back here!" I followed the commotion.

A white pickup was parked by Lisa's front gate, and Glen and Tim were walking toward us. The dogs broiled around them, yapping furiously.

"Joey, Rita, shut up!" Lisa shouted.

No response from the dogs. They kept barking and feinting, nipping at convenient heels. Lisa picked a boot off her front porch where it sat by the door and flung it at the tangle of dogs. She scored a direct hit on the blue one. He yipped and slunk over to her, looking guilty. Without support, the red dog yielded to another yell of, "Hush!"

"They don't like men." Lisa sighed. "I'm sure you can guess why. They know that's Dad's pickup and they shouldn't bark at him, but they do it anyway."

"Queenslands are like that," I said.

"But I feel safe with them, you know." Lisa smiled.

Glen and Tim had made it to the front porch by now, and Lisa ushered them into the house. The big orange cat wove in and out between them, greeting the newcomers. The Queenslands ignored the cat, except when they thought no one was looking and aimed quick, soft snaps in his direction.

Glen paid no attention to Lisa's menagerie, wading through them to sit down at the table and take the beer Lisa gave him. Tim cussed the dogs and cats impartially as he walked into the kitchen. "Worthless no-good sons of bitches."

"You always were a dog hater," Lisa shot at him.

"For God's sake, Lisa, every dog you own wants to bite me." Tim took the beer Lisa handed him and sat down at the table.

Lisa gestured gently at one of the two empty chairs, and I sat down, too. Lisa took the last chair. We were gathered.

"So, what's the problem?" Glen's face was drawn tight, fine lines of tension around his eyes. He looked old and tired, I thought. It was not something I was used to thinking of Glen.

Lisa produced the piece of cardboard and began the story; I hardly listened. I was watching Glen as circumspectly as I could, thinking about what he'd meant to me over the years, trying to sort out my feelings.

I didn't want to think of Glen as old and tired, I realized. He represented something that I was loath to let go of completely—a childhood memory of a time when I could safely look up to the adults around me, counting on them for help and guidance. That time was long past, but Glen remained, a remnant of my youth. I'd invested him with heroic properties, and I wasn't about to allow him to assume the guise of a mere mortal.

Lisa finished her story, "Now you can't say that was an accident."

Glen didn't say anything. Tim looked up from his beer. "You're being stupid, Lisa."

Lisa flashed at him, snapping like one of her dogs, "Well, how the hell do you think it happened, then?"

Tim shrugged. "I don't know. But what in the world would be the point of somebody doing that on purpose? They couldn't possibly know which horse would step in that hole."

Lisa fired right back at him. "They knew whatever happened, it would happen in Dad's arena. Somebody is trying to get at Dad."

Tim shook his head at her. "It still doesn't make sense, Lisa. If someone wants to get at Dad bad enough to risk killing somebody, why don't they take potshots at Dad himself? These things that happened are accidents; they don't fit a pattern. There isn't any motive that would explain them."

Glen spoke for the first time. "The hole Lisa saw wasn't dug by accident."

Tim gave him an easy look, almost indifferent. "Kids," he said, "fooling around. Trying to cause trouble."

Glen shrugged.

Lisa bristled. "Tim, that's ridiculous. Nobody, not even a kid as dumb as you were, could be stupid enough to do that and think it was just fun and games."

Tim grinned at her. Glen looked at me. "So what do you think, Gail?"

The ball was in my court. I cleared my throat. "I don't know, Glen. It does seem a little odd to me. Lisa's been telling me about it. I guess I'd have to say that I reserve judgment until I've got a few more facts."

Weak, weak, I told myself. But the natural outcome of my veterinary training. We veterinarians, like doctors, are loath to stick our necks out there on a long shot. Instead we run a few more tests, gather our facts.

Glen finished his beer in a long swallow and met my eyes. "Will you keep this to yourself?" he asked.

"Of course," I answered without thinking.

"Thank you." He stood up.

"Do you want to go down to the Saddlerack?" Lisa asked him. "I'm taking Gail out."

"No thanks," Glen said. "I need to get home." Glen's eyes were empty. What he was thinking God only knew.

"I'll go with you." Tim grinned at his sister.

Lisa gave him a dirty look, but it was too late. Glen turned and headed toward the door while Tim cocked his chair back a little more comfortably. "You might need some protection," he told Lisa.

I tried to decide if he was serious or not. It was hard to tell. Tim said everything, or almost everything, in a lazy, amused drawl. His brown eyes stayed sleepy and quiet. It was, I had to admit, a sexy expression. Tim looked as though he was think-ing of rolling into the sack any moment.

Lisa sighed. "I'm going to change my shirt," she said. "I'm filthy." She disappeared into the back of her house.

Tim and I sat at her table and looked at each other. I'd known Tim ever since high school, too. He was some four or five years younger than I, the same age as my longtime friend Bret Bon-cantini. Bret and Tim had been buddies, which had created a bond, fragile but tenuous, between me and Tim.

"So, how's Bret doing?" he asked me.

"OK, I guess; I haven't heard from him in a while. I guess you know Deb's pregnant?"

"Yeah, I heard."

Tim and I raised our eyebrows at each other in mutual amazement. To those who had known Bret's irreverent, irre-sponsible lifestyle, his announced decision a year ago to marry his off-again, on-again girlfriend, Deb, and retire to the Sierra Nevada foothills to raise cattle and children had come as some-thing of a shock. Nobody had believed he meant it. Appar-ently, though, we were wrong.

"Well, I wish him the best of luck." Tim sounded as though

he thought Bret would need it. I didn't argue. Raising a family, let alone a bunch of cattle, sounded like hard work to me.

Lisa came back into the kitchen with her springy curls damp. She wore a clean T-shirt and jeans, and her eyes were bright.

Tim gave a long wolf whistle. "You look pretty good for thirty-five."

She punched him in the shoulder. "Thirty-four. I'll be thirty-five next month. Come on; let's go. They've got an air conditioner at the Saddlerack."

I leaped to my feet with alacrity. I was more than ready for an air conditioner. Lisa's little house seemed to have gathered the stale heat of the afternoon; a drop of sweat ran down my cheek as I stood up.

Lisa shut the dogs in the yard, and we all piled into her pickup. Settling into the seat between her and Tim, as we jounced down the dirt road I was reminded of many, many high school evenings. How lighthearted they had been. A little of that feeling returned to me now, that sense of rolling down the road on a Saturday with the eager expectation that anything could happen next. With a jolt, I realized I'd forgotten all about Lonny. Lonny and Sara.

What the hell, I thought. By the time Lisa pulled into the parking lot of the Saddlerack some ten minutes later, I'd convinced myself that maybe I was ready to forget about Lonny permanently.

SEVEN

The Saddlerack sits at the junction of Lone Oak Road and Skyline Road and it, along with a store/gas station, is the town of Lone Oak. A couple of houses clustered nearby. Redwood trees shaded the buildings, making them look cool and welcoming this hot afternoon.

The little bar hadn't changed a bit since I'd seen it last. Shingled all over, with a tin roof and bright red trim, it hunkered cheerfully down by the side of the road. A fading sign announced: COLD BEER.

I was more interested in cold air. Tim pulled the door open and I walked through it, drinking in the cool, dim interior like a long swallow of spring water.

Lisa walked ahead of me into the bar half of the bar/restaurant and headed automatically for the round table in the corner. She pulled up short when she realized someone else was sitting there.

Susan Slater was sitting there. With the bespectacled man in shorts who had been with her at the roping. Their protest signs were on the floor at their feet, and they had mugs of draft beer in front of them.

Lisa started to do an abrupt about-face, but I grabbed her elbow firmly. "Come on," I hissed, and we marched up to the table together. "Mind if we sit down?" I asked.

Susan's companion looked at us blankly. Susan stared up into my face, narrowing her eyes. "Go right ahead. I'd like to talk to you."

We sat down in the two remaining chairs; I glanced around the room. Everything looked just the same. Old, battered trophy heads and faded, curling slogans covered the walls. The long wooden bar was scuffed to just the right degree of shabbiness. I recognized several local ranchers and ropers who had been at Glen's, standing or sitting, draft beers in hand.

Tim was ordering drinks from the bartender. My eyes snapped back for a second look. "That's Janey," I said.

Janey Borba, Al's daughter, had been in Lisa's and my high school class, along with Susan. And here she was, tending bar in the Saddlerack, seventeen years later.

She stood with her chin up, wearing the same belligerent expression she had worn in high school. Like Al, Janey always seemed to have a grudge against the world. Her mouth stayed straight and hard as Tim smiled at her, and her big, dark eyes never flickered. Janey hadn't changed a bit.

She'd kept her figure, and it was the kind you saw mostly on *Playboy* centerfolds. Her bright red T-shirt was tight enough to show off her nipples, and her jeans looked like they were painted on. The general effect was that of a billboard shouting, Come hither.

But above all this lavishly displayed temptation rode Janey's face. Taken feature by feature, it was attractive enough, but in contrast to her clothes, her expression said, *Don't mess with me, buster.* Her long black hair fell to her waist, but she wore it pulled back in a severe braid, which only highlighted her stern expression. Everything from the upward tilt of her chin to the thin-lipped line of her mouth announced that she could take care of any unwanted overtures.

Susan had followed my eyes to Janey and was staring at her. "I don't get it," she said. "Why does she dress like that?" Susan's voice was loud enough to carry easily to where Janey stood, but not a muscle flickered in Janey's face.

I shrugged. I'd never been friends with Janey Borba, but I had no wish to insult the woman.

Susan wasn't easily put off. "She's never liked men, so why dress like that?"

"Everybody's got different taste," I said softly, watching Tim try to flirt with Janey. She gave him cold looks in exchange for his suggestive ones, put his beer and his change on the counter, and walked away. Tim watched the red T-shirt and skintight jeans undulate away from him with obvious regret.

Lisa sighed in my ear. "That damn Tim's been trying to get in her pants for years. I don't know why he bothers. Janey won't give him the time of day." All this was said in an obvious whisper to me while Lisa looked pointedly away from Susan.

Susan glared openly back. Maybe sitting these two down together hadn't been such a good idea.

"So what did you want to talk to me about?" I asked Susan.

"How you, a supposedly ethical veterinarian, can condone something as cruel and inhumane as team roping." Once again, Susan's tone was such that everyone in the bar could listen in. I noticed a certain stillness fall over the room at her words.

Lisa stirred next to me, and I put a hand on her arm. "Why exactly is it you think team roping is cruel and inhumane?" I asked Susan.

"That's obvious," she snapped, "to any halfway moral person. Those poor horses and cows."

"Have you ever owned a horse or a cow?"

"Well, no." Susan was wary. "But I know cruelty when I see it."

"I'm not sure you do, though. How do you think horses want to live?"

"Horses, like all animals, should live free. We humans have no right to make slaves out of them." Susan declaimed this in the pitch of a public orator. It was clear she'd made the statement before. Her male friend was watching her with a look of admiration.

"Susan, that's impossible," I said. "There isn't enough range left for all horses to run free. The wild horses that do exist are being captured and locked up in pens because they're overgrazing the land they're on. Various environmental groups are protesting their very existence; they say the horses are destroying the native habitat. On top of which, I do not think any horse would rather be starving to death in a poor year or dying of infection or packing a broken leg until some cougar gets him. I think horses are, or can be, happier in the company of men."

"Horses do not want to be slaves," she protested.

"I'm not sure what you mean by a slave. Are dogs and cats slaves? Do you think they should run free, too?"

"Ideally, all animals would be free and equal to humans."

"Ideally, huh? How about practically? Do you just want to turn all the horses and dogs and cats in the world loose to romp around in traffic?"

Lisa grinned at this, but Susan bounced right back. "Of course not, but I do not want to see horses and cattle tortured."

"Do you think horses and cattle would rather stand around in a pen all day than go team roping?"

"They'd rather be in a pasture," she said firmly.

"They might. In a perfect world, all horses might live in big pastures and run around and eat grass all day. In a perfect world, we'd all be rich and have no troubles. In real life, most people can't afford to own a hundred acres for every horse. The best we can do is provide them with a decent-sized pen. And horses like to get out of their pen and go do something where they run hard. It's their nature."

"How do you know that?" she demanded.

I was silent for a second. This was the problem. If you knew horses, you knew these things, but how to explain them to a non-horseman?

Before I could formulate the words, Lisa jumped in. "Susan, everybody knows that. If you're so goddamn ignorant about horses you should keep your mouth shut."

Susan's eyes flashed fire. Before she could open her mouth, I said, "Wait a minute. Just listen. The reason Lisa said that is she's spent her whole life around horses. She knows them. Susan, do you have a cat or a dog?"

"Yes," she admitted. "Both."

"Well, you know if your dog or cat is hungry or feeling friendly or wants to go out or feels sick or whatever, don't you?"

"Sure."

"Well, Lisa knows that about horses and cattle. We both know if our horses are enjoying what they're doing, and many, not all, team-roping horses like their work."

"They don't like breaking their legs," Susan shot back.

"No," I agreed. "But I can tell you for a fact, most broken legs occur at home in the corral or pasture, when a horse gets kicked by another horse. And that would happen to horses living in the wild, too. The only difference would be the horse would suffer for days, maybe weeks."

"That horse this morning broke his leg because some dumb person was roping on him," she argued.

"I suppose you could say that. But it's as likely that you'll get killed in a traffic accident on the way to the store as a horse will break its leg in that situation. Are you going to quit driving because of that?" I watched Susan closely.

She didn't say a word, just looked confused. If she knew about the hole, if she'd dug it even, her features gave no clue.

Lisa saw an opportunity in the silence. "Why don't you just leave us alone?" she said to Susan. "Dad and I aren't cruel to animals. Nobody on the ranch is."

"That's bullshit," Susan said. "I see you using those electric cattle prods on the poor cattle all the time."

"Susan, cattle prods are not cruel," I said. "Cattle have to be moved through chutes occasionally, even if they aren't roping cattle. They need their vaccinations; they need to be doctored if they're hurt. Cattle prods are the most humane way to do it. Otherwise, people would have to beat on the cattle with sticks and whips, which would be much harder on them."

"How would you like being electrocuted with all those volts?" she demanded.

"Six volts." Tim's lazy drawl came from behind us. He was sitting at the bar, listening to our conversation, as was everybody else in the room. "Hand me that thing," he said over his shoulder to Janey.

Janey produced a hotshot from behind the bar; no doubt, I thought, it was a handy weapon for a woman to squelch a drunken bar fight.

Tim held the hotshot in one hand and spoke in his usual slow, quiet voice to Susan. "Hotshots are humane, like Gail says. They don't hurt the cattle. Watch." And Tim pressed the prongs into his palm and pushed the button.

The hotshot buzzed audibly in the sudden stillness. Tim sat quietly for five seconds, taking the jolt without a flicker, then put the hotshot back on the bar. "See?" he said evenly. "No big deal."

Even Susan was silenced. We all stared at Tim. I knew what the hotshot would feel like; I'd touched electric fences before— by accident. It wasn't pleasant.

Tim looked unaffected. I had no idea how much was pose and how much genuine toughness. Lisa shook her head at her brother in amusement and exasperation, then turned back to Susan, once again on the fight. "We really aren't cruel to our animals, OK?"

Susan was still staring at Tim. She shifted her gaze to Lisa, then back to me. "Gail, do you really think team roping is a humane, ethical thing to do to animals?" For the first time in the conversation, Susan sounded as if she was honestly asking a question, not just pontificating.

"I think, like most everything else in life, it depends on the circumstances," I told her. "It isn't black or white."

Lisa's eyes shot to my face in protest, and I said firmly, "No, Lisa, I'm not going to say team roping's always wonderful for the animals. I've seen plenty of ropers be cruel to horses and cattle; I've seen unnecessary harm done. But it doesn't have to be that way."

I looked Susan in the eye. "I have problems with some aspects of roping. I hate to see cattle or horses get hurt. I don't like calf roping, for instance; I've seen too many calves break their necks or legs. In the case of team roping, I think it's important what rules the arena has. Glen has the most humane rules of any place I've been. The header undallies when he faces, which means the steers don't get a hard jerk, and there's a no-drag rule, which means if a steer goes down, the header has to let him get up. On top of which, Glen takes really good care of the cattle. He feeds them well and doctors them if they're sick and doesn't rope them too often. All that stuff's important."

"What about the horses?"

"That has a lot to do with who owns them. Some people are kind to their horses and care for them well and don't run too many steers on them, and I think those horses are mostly happy to go roping. Some people are hard on their horses, and those horses are miserable. Some people beat their wives and children, too."

The room was completely silent. "We do love our horses," I said at last. "Lisa and Glen and I, and lots of other people you see out there roping. I think, Susan, if you want to talk about cruelty to horses, you better start by buying a horse of your own and learning what they're like."

"And in the meantime," Lisa added sharply, "Leave Dad alone."

I glared at Lisa. She seemed absolutely bent on antagonizing Susan. For her part, Susan got to her feet, looking pissed off and confused all at once. "Come on," she said to her friend. "We're going home."

Obediently he picked up the protest signs and followed her to the door. Susan turned back to give the room a final comment, but her voice was drowned out by the deeper, stronger tones of a voice from the bar: "Get the hell out of here, you lousy bitch." The speaker stared right at Susan. "And don't come back."

EIGHT

Susan looked about to protest, then whirled and left the room without a word, skirt swirling, companion in tow. Charles Domini took a long swallow of his beer and surveyed the bar. "Good riddance," he said plainly.

Charles looked drunk to me. When Charles got drunk, Charles got mean. This was common knowledge in Lone Oak. Charles Domini owned the only other big ranch in the area; the Domini Ranch had been around as long as the Bennett Ranch.

The difference was that Charles, unlike Glen, was not popular with the locals. Charles was too prone to being drunk and mean, and his ranch was run-down and untended. Periodically he logged a portion of it or sold some more off to developers. This made him rich, but it did not make him popular. I didn't know anyone who liked Charles Domini.

He sat in the middle of a small group of people, which included several rough-looking men and his wife, Pat. The men all seemed pleased at Charles's statement. Pat looked disgusted.

I'd known Pat for years, and I had never figured out what she was doing with Charles. His money seemed the only possible attraction. And yet I would have thought better of her.

A slim, attractive woman somewhere in her forties or fifties, Pat had smooth brown skin, a loose cap of ruffled brown curls, and friendly eyes. She was capable with horses and cattle and roped a good deal better than her husband, who preferred kibitizing at the arena fence. Rumor had it that Pat and Glen were having an affair.

These rumors had been going on for twenty years. I had no idea if they were true. I had never seen Pat and Glen act anything more than polite to each other. I sometimes thought it was just the fact that they were both such attractive people, with spouses who were a good deal less appealing, that had fueled all the talk.

Tim got up from the bar and came and sat down at the table with Lisa and me, putting two draft beers in front of us. "Thought you might need something to cool your throat after all that talk," he said to me with a grin.

"Thanks," I said. "That was quite a stunt with the hotshot."

Tim shrugged. He had taken a chair against the wall, and he leaned back in it. His brown eyes drifted around the room and then stopped. I followed his gaze to where Al Borba sat by himself at the end of the bar, drink in hand.

Al stared at the mirror behind the bar, his face sullen and withdrawn. To all intents and purposes, he appeared unaware that anyone was in the room with him. Occasionally he took a sip of his drink. Janey stood behind the bar opposite him, her chin tilted up, her eyes watchful. Neither of them spoke.

"Why does your dad keep him around?" I asked Lisa. "I've always wondered. It's not like he acts any nicer to Glen."

Lisa had no trouble guessing what I was talking about. "I know," she said. "He gives me the creeps. He never says a word to me if he can help it. But Dad just says he's a good worker and he sees no reason to let Al go. Al and Janey both live in that mobile home by the roping arena. Janey's always lived with her dad." Lisa shook her head. "Al's father worked for my granddad when Dad was a little boy. Al's just kind of a fixture."

"He's an asshole." Tim's lazy tone didn't change, but Lisa and I looked at him cautiously. There was an undercurrent there, something that was hard to place.

Tim's eyes moved on down the bar from Al and rested on Pat Domini in a speculative way. I wondered briefly if Tim was considering going into competition with his father. If so, he was going to have a rough time of it tonight, as Charles stood right next to Pat, his arm resting on the bar beside her. Pat ignored her husband.

A big man with olive skin and dark eyes and hair, Charles was talking loudly in a definite voice, waving one hand with a massive gold ring on it, making some important point. Now Charles, I thought, was an asshole.

He finished his point and, as if feeling eyes upon him, turned to look at the three of us. Lisa and I looked away, but Tim kept his gaze steady, staring straight at Charles. Charles smiled slowly, not a pleasant smile. Then he edged his way out of the group and came walking over to our table.

A long time before he reached us it was clear he was not just a little drunk; he was very drunk. The smile on his face was matched by his unfocused eyes. I sighed. This could be trouble. Glancing at Tim, I saw he looked pleased. Great.

Lisa shot Tim a sidelong look. "Don't get in a fight, Tim, huh?"

Tim didn't say a word, just kept meeting Charles's eyes.

Domini finished the trip up to our table and stood staring down at Tim with the same silly, unpleasant grin. Tim cocked his chair back a little and looked up into the older man's face. Tim wore a bright blue BENNETT RANCH baseball cap, and he tipped it farther back on his head as if to get a better view.

"Howdy, Charles," he said. The lazy drawl was almost an insult in itself.

Such subtleties were lost on Domini. He rocked slightly from side to side as he stood over Tim, grinning down at him. "Howdy, Mr. Big Shot Bennett," Charles said. I sighed inwardly. Charles continued, "Son of the original Big Shot Bennett, who is only the biggest asshole in Santa Cruz County. Maybe in the state of California. I'd have to give it some thought."

Not a muscle twitched in Tim's face. He cocked his chair a little farther back. He looked completely relaxed. I wasn't fooled.

"Now why would you say that, Charles?" Tim said in a soft, friendly voice.

"Because it's true." Charles's voice was getting louder. Various people turned to stare at us. Tim looked as unconcerned as usual. Charles went on. "Your asshole of a father thinks his shit don't stink. He thinks he can do anything he wants to do and no one can stop him. Well, he's wrong. He's gonna find that out. He can be stopped, all right. He's just a dumb prick."

On the last words, I sensed the sudden coil of muscle in Tim, like a wound spring, heard the click of his chair legs hitting the floor, tensed myself to grab him. Domini took a step back and cocked his arm; it was clear to him that he'd provoked a fight. In the split second before our motionless group could erupt into a shambles of lunging men, spilled beer, and overturned tables, Pat fairly leaped between Tim and Charles.

She grabbed Charles by the arm and put her body squarely in front of his. I caught a whiff of her perfume, which reminded me of jasmine, and I felt the tension ebb out of Tim. His chair tipped back again. I relaxed. I heard Lisa let out a long breath next to me.

Pat looked at Tim. "I'm sorry," she said flatly. "I didn't notice what he was up to." Then she looked at Charles. "You've had too much to drink, dear," she said with a totally phony sweetness. "I think we'd better go home."

Charles didn't seem to be mentally organized enough to argue. Pat grabbed his arm and pushed him toward the door. She gave us an apologetic smile over one shoulder as they disappeared through it.

"I like Pat," Lisa said abruptly. "I sure wish Dad had married her instead of Joyce."

"There's just the slight problem of that asshole she's married to," Tim drawled.

"There's such a thing as divorce," Lisa told him.

Tim swiveled his eyes to meet hers. There was a sudden un-Tim-like intensity in them. But he spoke in his usual slow, relaxed way. "Well, Pat might divorce old Charles, I'll agree to that. But Dad will never in a million years divorce Joyce." The bitterness in Tim's voice surprised me. "He won't do it because he's more interested in his stupid goddamn pride than he is in anything else. A messy divorce wouldn't make him look good. He'd rather suffer on like some kind of martyr than lose face."

Lisa looked as startled as I felt. "But, Tim," she said carefully, "everybody knows about him and Pat. What's the difference?"

"The difference is that he doesn't think everybody knows. Has he ever admitted to you or me or anybody else that he has a thing going with Pat? No. Do we even really know for sure they've got something going?"

Lisa shrugged.

"We don't," Tim said. "Dad just goes on thinking he looks like the ultimate in upright, moral behavior. The great Glen Bennett, pillar of the community." Tim's voice was angry and sarcastic, and it stunned both Lisa and me to silence. Tim got up abruptly and walked over to the bar.

Lisa looked at me. "That wasn't like him."

"No," I agreed.

"Why do you think he's so down on Dad?" Lisa sounded confused.

"I don't know. I haven't seen much of Tim in years. And we've never known each other all that well."

Inwardly, though, I wondered if I didn't understand. Glen had always been larger than life; I wasn't the only one who'd admired him. Rich, successful, handsome, charming with women, respected by men . . . almost a king in his little kingdom.

And Tim was supposed to be the crown prince. Tim was almost thirty and had never had a job—just helped his dad with the ranch. At some level, even though he wouldn't show it, he must be fighting out his own terms of adulthood. And maybe finding it impossible to do with this improbable hero of a father always looming over him, making whatever he did seem small and insignificant. Maybe he just needed to find some holes in Glen, chop him down to size, make him seem human. If Tim could make Glen seem small, Tim could feel bigger.

I watched Tim standing at the bar in his loose, relaxed slouch, waiting for Janey to walk over to him. Even as Glen stood square and straight, shoulders back, head up, Tim had looked just the opposite ever since I'd known him. Shambling, humorous, spine in an easy curve, an obvious reluctance to take anything seriously—that was Tim.

It did occur to me to wonder how deep Tim's resentment might go. Then I dropped the thought. I could not picture Tim digging holes in Glen's arena.

Tim came back over to our table, beer in hand. His usual easy grin was back in place.

"Getting anywhere with Janey?" I asked him.

"Never do," he said. "She's meaner than cat shit. I don't know why I bother. Now that's more like it," he added.

Lisa and I followed his glance. Coming in the door at the far end of the bar were two girls. They looked barely old enough to be in the bar, and both had lush, overripe bodies that seemed about to spill out of their tight clothes. Taking lessons from Janey, I thought cynically. Lisa rolled her eyes.

Tim arched his eyebrows at her. "I'll take the one in the pink top," he said.

Lisa looked at him in exasperation. "For God's sake, Tim. The one in the pink top is Tony Alvarez's new wife. They just got married a year ago. You want to get shot? That's Tony's cousin over there, next to Danny Bell."

Tim shrugged. "Watch this," he said.

He ambled across the bar to where the two girls were settling themselves on bar stools and managed to end up seated between them. Pretty quick we could hear a laughing argument over who would buy the drinks.

"Now that is really stupid," Lisa said. "It'd serve him right if he did get shot. Those girls aren't worth it."

I had to agree with her. The girls looked young and dumb, their hair frothing in elaborate perms, their faces heavily made up. Both of them seemed prone to giggling. I felt a little sad as I looked at them.

Lisa met my eyes. "Makes you feel old, huh?"

"Yeah, it does. Though I hope I was never *that* young and dumb."

"We were, though. Or at least I was. Sometimes I wish I could go back, start over, be young again. Make different choices."

I thought about it. "I wouldn't be young again," I told her.

Lisa smiled sadly. "I might. Maybe I'd pick a better man this time and end up happily married."

"You still could," I pointed out.

"I don't know. I feel like it's all passed me by. That girl Tim's trying to hustle, the one who just married Tony, that's Bob White's daughter. I used to baby-sit her. I was twenty-four when she was ten years old. It makes me feel ancient."

I punched her lightly on the arm. "Just start looking at older men," I teased, and was immediately sorry.

"You mean like Lonny Peterson?" Lisa sounded mischievous. "I always thought he was attractive. So, when are you two getting hitched?"

The question was too much for my fragile equilibrium. "Not in the foreseeable future." I tried to keep my tone light but knew the edge was there.

63

"Oh."

I could tell Lisa felt she'd said the wrong thing and hastened to reassure her. "It's no big deal. Things aren't going too well right now, that's all."

"Is it something you want to talk about?"

"Hell, Lisa, I don't know. Lonny's seeing his wife again."

"You mean he's not divorced?" Lisa sounded surprised.

"No. Separated, but not divorced."

Someone had put a quarter in the jukebox, and the opening bars of "Amarillo by Morning" drifted around the room. Once again I felt like crying. Shaking my head hard, I told Lisa, "I guess I don't really want to talk about it."

"OK. Are you ready for dinner?"

"You bet."

I followed her into the restaurant section of the building, squeezed into a narrow booth across from her, and ordered a steak. It seemed appropriate. All through dinner, Lisa kept up a running monologue, mostly about her father's horse-breeding program and the colts she was starting for him. As we had coffee, I told her about my two horses, Plumber and Gunner, both six years old this year, how I was just starting to rope on Gunner and how I was having trouble getting Plumber sound. I'd operated on him twice now for a fractured sesamoid bone, an injury that had been the reason I acquired him, but this time I was sure I had the problem solved and would be riding the horse this summer.

On and on we chatted, the touchy subjects of Lonny and Glen and the stalker forgotten for the moment, horses providing both of us with a means to reestablish our old friendship. A common interest in horses had drawn us together as teenagers, and that same interest ran equally strong now that we were adults. It made a bond—a bond I could feel we were renewing.

Eventually Lisa excused herself to go to the bathroom, disappearing through the door of the bar. I stared after her, thinking aimless thoughts: how good it felt to chat to another woman this way, how much I enjoyed talking to Lonny about horses, how fragile happiness was. Strains of the gently melancholic song "Pancho and Lefty" wafted out the bar entrance. I could hear the rumble of male voices, the heavy sound of laughter.

Lisa reappeared in the doorway; I started to smile, but the smile froze on my face. Lisa looked like a ghost—drawn-faced, drained of color, terrified.

"Gail, come on; let's go. Tim's getting a ride home. I need to go." She hurried through the words.

I stared at her, still not comprehending this sudden change, but she had already turned and was heading out the door. I got up and followed her.

She was in her pickup when I got outside, and I opened the passenger door and climbed in.

"Lock it," she said, her voice brusque.

"Lisa, what is going on?" I asked as I obediently pushed the lock down.

She stared straight ahead through the windshield, eyes riveted on the doorway, tension plain in every line of her face and body. "Sonny just walked in that bar," she said.

NINE

Sonny Santos? Your ex?"

"Yeah, him." Lisa started the truck and began backing out of the parking lot.

"Wait a minute," I said.

"Why?"

"I want to get a look at him."

"What in hell for?"

"Lisa," I said gently, "I know this is hard for you, but if you really are worried that Sonny's stalking your dad, and you really think I can help, I need to be able to at least recognize Sonny if I see him."

"Gail, I can't go in there. I can't be around him."

"OK. Just sit out here. Keep the doors locked. It won't take me a minute."

Lisa started to protest, then said, "He has black hair, and he's wearing a blue shirt."

I got out of the truck. "I'll be right back," I told her.

Marching firmly to the door, I pulled it open and walked into the bar. Heads turned at my entrance; curious glances came my way. Ordinary curious glances, the sort that are directed at any newcomer entering a bar. I scanned the room.

Tim still sat at the counter with the two girls he'd spotted earlier and barely looked at me. Al Borba was in his accustomed place. Janey stood behind the bar; her eyes ran over me dispassionately, the steady, practical, aloof eyes of a bartender. I had no idea if she recognized me or not. Three men in a group, too old to be Sonny, two younger men whom I'd seen at the roping today at a table—they weren't Sonny, either.

But at the table in the corner, the table where Lisa and I had been sitting, was a dark man in a white straw cowboy hat and light blue shirt. He had the high cheekbones and hard-planed face that came with a predominantly Spanish lineage, and he was every bit as good-looking as Lisa had said. And even from across the room, he seemed arrogant as hell.

I knew a little bit about Sonny Santos. Anyone who had anything to do with team roping had heard of him. He came from a famous rodeo family; both his father and brother had been national champions, so Sonny had been raised in a world where he was royalty. Not only that, but he'd fulfilled tradition by becoming a national champion himself. It didn't surprise me that he looked arrogant.

Sonny raised his eyes from his drink and met my stare. His own gaze was dark and cold—appraising, dismissive, callous. I wasn't young and good-looking enough for him. No question about it; in his mind I was just another woman who would like to take him home. He looked away.

I smiled quietly to myself, scanned the bar once more as if I were looking for someone, shrugged slightly, and turned and went out the door.

Lisa was still in her pickup, and the engine was running. She flicked the locked door open when I reached for the handle. As soon as I was inside, she pulled out of the parking lot and started down Lone Oak Road.

"Did you see him?"

"Yeah, I saw him. He is good-looking."

"A good-looking bastard."

"Do you really think he's behind your accidents?"

"I don't know. Sonny is a strange man. The only thing he cares about is his pride. I can still see the look on his face when Dad ran him off that night; it really scares me."

I thought about it. Sonny Santos might just be the kind of person who considered himself above any laws of human behavior. If Lisa and Glen, between them, had upset his private fantasy of Sonny as God, maybe it was possible that he would go to some trouble to avenge himself.

"I don't know, Lisa," I said at last. "Who else could it be, if it's not him?"

"Susan?" She shrugged. And then, slowly, "Or Charles Domini, maybe."

"Charles? Charles has been around here forever. Why would he suddenly start bothering Glen?"

"I'm not sure. I always thought Charles was mostly hot air. And Dad's thing with Pat, if it is a thing, has been going on for years. But Charles seemed different tonight—more hostile. And one thing I can tell you: Charles can be violent."

"Yeah, I know. I've seen him get in fistfights before. But that's not the same as stalking someone."

"It's more than that." Lisa was talking quietly, as if to herself. "Charles can be vicious. We gathered cattle on his ranch once. Charles and I ended up riding this one field together, just by accident. There was a dog trotting across the field, a little dog, a beagle or something, and Charles pulled a pistol out of his saddlebag and shot him."

I sighed. "Lisa, a lot of ranchers will shoot a dog that's in with their cattle. They have a legal right to do it."

"Gail, I know that. I was raised in this country, remember? It wasn't like that. This little dog was just trotting across the field, minding his own business; there weren't any cattle in sight. When Charles got that pistol out of his saddlebag, I was shocked. Still, like you said, it was his legal right. Nobody else I know would have shot the dog; he was clearly somebody's pet on his way home, and not the type of dog who usually chases cattle. But Charles got the gun out and he had this grin on his face. The same grin he had tonight when he was trying to start a fight with Tim. I swear to God, Gail, I was afraid to say anything to him. Before I could get up my nerve, he shot the dog. Not to kill. He shot one of the dog's legs off."

I could see the scene in my mind, the little dog crying, the blood spurting, Charles grinning. I felt sick.

"He did it on purpose," Lisa said quietly. "He's a real good shot. He took a while to finish killing that dog. He was enjoying himself. That's what he looked like tonight when he was heckling Tim. He didn't act like a dumb drunk trying to pick a fight. He acted smug, happy, like he was enjoying it."

We were both quiet. I tried to visualize Charles Domini digging holes in Glen's arena. It didn't seem likely.

We were rolling down the mountain road now, nearing the town of Corralitos. "So where do you live?" Lisa asked.

"In Soquel. Up Old San Jose Road."

I could see her nod, in the faint light from the dashboard. Soquel was a half hour away. We made the drive in silence. Neither Lisa nor I seemed inclined to break it.

When she pulled in my driveway, I felt a slight reluctance to get out of the truck. In one short day, Lisa and her problems had become a part of my life. Lisa seemed to feel the same way. The look she turned on me verged on pleading, "Come on up to the ranch tomorrow, Gail, please. We're going to gather. You can help us. That is, if you're not busy," she added belatedly.

Busy. No, I wasn't busy that I knew of. I had this whole weekend off. And, for all I was aware, by tomorrow Sara might be moved back in with Lonny. Great thought.

"My horses are out at Lonny's," I told Lisa. "And he owns the rig that hauls them. I don't exactly want to ask him for a favor right now."

"No problem. You can ride Chester."

"Chester?"

"He's the little bay I was heeling on today. You'll like him. He's a real sweetheart. Dad raised him. He's by Smoke and out of Dad's best mare. Say you'll come, Gail."

Why not? It was better than sitting around waiting for Lonny to call. "All right," I said. "What time?"

"Eight o'clock." Lisa gave me a brief young-Lisa smile. "See you then." And she pulled out of my driveway.

I walked slowly to my front door. Time was, I would have heard the welcome jingle of Blue's collar on the other side as I put the key in the lock. No more. Blue was gone. I still couldn't get used to it. Without Blue, the house didn't feel like home.

Unlocking the door, I let myself inside. Everything looked neat and clean—too neat and clean. I'd scrubbed my humble cabin to within an inch of its life yesterday. My friend Denise Hennessy, a realtor, was showing it to prospective buyers this weekend.

It wasn't that I disliked the little house. It was just that the steep, shady quarter of an acre it was located on was no place to keep horses or have a garden—two things I was set on doing. It was my good luck that real estate prices in Santa Cruz County had risen so spectacularly during the four years I'd owned the house that the property was now worth double what I'd paid for it. My profit would be enough (I hoped) for a sizable down payment on a bigger place.

Walking to the table, I picked up the note Denise had left me: "I showed it to three parties today. One of them, a single woman, a high school teacher, seemed very interested. It looks good. Will be in touch."

Well, well, well. I surveyed the house with the eyes of a

stranger, wondering if this schoolteacher would be moved to make an offer. Short sandy beige carpet set off the curved shapes of my few pieces of antique furniture and harmonized gently with the soft-white walls and oiled wood window and door trim. Both living room and kitchen were tiny (the bathroom was even more so) but cozy and comfortable-looking, and that was all there was to the upper story.

Sighing, I set my hands and feet on the rungs of the ladder that was my stairway and lowered myself through a hole in the kitchen floor. Since the house was built on a steep bank on the edge of Soquel Creek, it had two levels. The upper story was at street level, and the smaller, basementlike lower story was at creek level, more or less. Very much creek level in a wet winter, I'd found. Someone had had the bright idea of connecting the two stories with a ladder. It was space-efficient but could be a little awkward.

Down below was my bedroom. I could hear the murmur of the creek outside in the darkness through an open window as I began undressing for bed. Would someone else be undressing here in a month or so? And where would I be?

I felt lost and disoriented at the thought, and very alone. Everything was changing. Blue was gone; my house was soon to be gone; Lonny was perhaps going.

You've got your job, I reminded myself, and your horses— you'll be fine. You're used to being alone. So how come it felt so shitty right now?

A loud meow broke into my wallow in self-pity, and a fluffy grayish tabby cat with white paws and chest and a lynxlike face jumped through the open window and onto the bed. "Hello, Bonner," I said.

I rubbed the cat's head and scratched the base of his tail; he arched his back and purred, and I felt suddenly better. As I pulled the covers over me, the cat settled down by my side, a warm, steady weight, purring contentedly. "Who needs a man," I told him.

I'll get another dog, I added to myself, as soon as I get moved. One of Lisa's puppies maybe. And I'll have the horses with me. On these comforting thoughts, I fell asleep, Glen and his stalker the last thing on my mind, happily unaware of what the coming days would bring.

TEN

I pulled up at Lisa's front gate at eight o'clock the next morning. Joey and Rita barked vociferously on the other side of the picket fence, and I regarded them with even more interest than I had the day before.

Joe was a "blue" heeler, like my old dog, Blue, a color that was really more of a mottled gray. He had the same square, sturdy frame, the same bobbed tail, and would be about the same weight—thirty pounds, more or less. The Harlequinesque appearance his half-mask gave him was immediately engaging, at least to someone who likes Queenslands.

Rita was smaller and shyer; when I opened the gate and let myself in the yard, she kept her distance, barking and occasionally aiming fake snaps in the direction of my heels. I could bite you, she was telling me, don't do anything wrong.

I walked steadily to the front porch, the dogs accompanying me, still barking, but in an accepting rather than an angry tone. Lisa opened the door and smiled at me. "They like you," she said.

"I like Queenslands. They probably know it. I think I do want a pup," I added.

"Good. I'll save the pick of the litter for you. Come on in and have a cup of coffee."

I followed Lisa into the house, and the big orange cat appeared from nowhere and began weaving between my legs.

"Hi, Zip," I said. He stood up on his back legs and put his front paws on my thigh, just like a dog, and I scratched his wide head.

Lisa handed me a cup of coffee, and I sat down in a fat, comfortable chair. Lisa settled herself on the couch with a cup of her own. The red dog jumped up next to her and put her head on Lisa's lap. To my surprise, the blue dog marched over and parked himself against my feet. He gave me a glance over his shoulder that said, as plain as words, "Don't go thinking you can pet me; I just happen to want to sit here, that's all."

"So, what's the program?" I asked Lisa.

"Oh, Dad will be by here when he's ready to start. We're shipping all the steers at the end of the week, so the whole ranch has to be gathered. The feed's gone. It wasn't a very good year, and this hot spell really finished it off."

I nodded. It was already warm at eight o'clock; we weren't done with the hot weather yet.

"Anyway, we're just gonna gather the home pasture today. With four of us, it'll be easy. We'll be done by lunch." Lisa sounded businesslike and carefree; the scared, dependent mood of last night vanished as if it had never been.

"What about your stalker?" I asked her. "Any new thoughts?"

"No. But things seem a lot better in the morning."

"They always do."

We smiled at each other. Suddenly both dogs lifted their heads and pricked their ears forward. The red dog woofed softly from her seat on the couch. Before they could do anything else, Lisa said firmly, "Don't bark. If you bark, you've had it."

They both gave her disappointed looks, but they were quiet. Lisa and I looked out the window. A dark green pickup appeared over the hill and drove down into the little valley, going fast.

"Tim's up early," Lisa commented. "For him, anyway."

Tim braked and slid the truck up to the gate. The pickup had a number 6 with a circle around it painted on both doors with white paint. Tim got out and started toward the front porch.

Whatever he'd been up to last night, it was clear it hadn't turned out too well. He had a black eye and a fat lip, his face looked puffy and bruised, and he was limping.

Lisa got up and opened the door for him. "So what happened to you?" she asked.

"Uh, I tripped and hit my face on the bar."

Lisa rolled her eyes. "Why lie?"

Tim laughed.

"Ralph Alvarez and his buddies beat the shit out of you for trying to pick up on Tony's wife, didn't they?" Lisa demanded.

"Tony helped, too," Tim said. He ran his tongue around the inside of his mouth. "I think I've still got all my teeth. I'm surprised, though." His eyes laughed at the two of us. "Tony happened to pull in right when I was rolling 'round with her in the backseat of her car. Boy, was that a scene. She had her shirt off, and he's jumping in there trying to drag me out and she's screaming and people are pouring out of the bar. Tony and I are slugging it out and she's standing there yelling with those great big bare boobs out in the parking lot for everyone to see."

Tim laughed and then winced. "My mouth doesn't work too good right now. I think four different guys had a shot at adjusting it. How 'bout some coffee?"

Lisa went into the kitchen to get him a cup, and he sat down in the remaining empty chair. "You here to help us gather?" he asked me.

"Sure." I watched him accept a cup of coffee from his sister, his beaten face as outwardly relaxed as ever. Tim was an odd one. For all his happy-go-lucky air, there was a strange streak of violence in him. That stunt with the hotshot yesterday, and his effort at picking a fight with Charles. Not to mention the diatribe about his father. And now this. For the first time, I allowed myself to seriously wonder whether Tim could be Lisa's stalker.

As impossible as it seemed on first blush, he had all the credentials, really. Resenting one's father could go very deep; human history was thick with bloody stories built on that theme. Tim lived here on the ranch; he knew all about horses and cattle and tractors and trailers—it was possible, I told myself.

And it would kill Glen if it was true. I looked over at Lisa. Maybe she was wrong about all this. Maybe these were accidents after all, just a string of coincidental bad luck.

Lisa was staring down at her cup of coffee, and I studied the neat, definite features under the blond curls. If Lisa was creating a stalker out of thin air, it pointed at a paranoia as extreme as the acts would be psychotic—if they were real. If Tim was Lisa's stalker, he was a very sick person, and if Lisa was making the stalker up, she was pretty darn sick herself. Neither scenario was pleasant to contemplate.

Tim took a long swallow of coffee, winced, and put a hand to his jaw. "Old Tony Alvarez was kind of upset," he said to the room at large.

"Who else got involved?" I asked him.

"Oh, Ralph, and Danny Bell."

"Not Sonny Santos?"

Lisa's head jerked up at the question; her eyes shot to her brother's face.

"Nah." Tim shook his head. "That bastard was gone before it happened. Had one drink and then left. Probably hoping for a glimpse of Lisa."

Nobody said anything.

"There was one funny thing, though," Tim went on slowly. "When Tony jumped on me it was no more than what I expected, and I wasn't surprised when Ralph and Danny joined in. I was sure getting the worst of it, though. Some of the other guys were trying to pull them off, but I could hear this big voice yelling, 'Let 'em fight.'

"People were yelling back, saying these guys were killing me, and by then I was just sort of rolling around, taking one punch after another. Finally they got Ralph and Danny pulled off, but Tony was coming back in for more, and I could still hear this voice yelling, 'Let 'em fight.'

"And suddenly it got to me. That was Al's voice. I looked up—even as out of it as I was, it shocked me enough to wake me up—and Al was looking down at me and smiling. Shit, he never smiles. He saw me look at him and his face closed down right away, but I saw that smile. He looked like he was gloating. I couldn't believe it. Hell, that bastard hates me. I don't know why.

"Then I started thinking about all this shit that's been happening, and how Lisa keeps saying it's not accidents. And I can't get the idea out of my mind. What if it's Al?"

Lisa and I stared at Tim. What she was thinking I didn't know. I wondered whether Tim was telling the truth or trying to cast suspicion on someone else. Either way, I didn't like it. A tangle of dark emotions seemed to be gathering around the Bennett family, and I felt inextricably caught in the net.

Lisa jumped to her feet. "Come on, let's go on down to the barn. Dad must be ready by now."

Tim and I followed her out the door. I felt a sudden intense worry about Glen. Where was he? Was he all right?

We piled into Tim's green truck, Joey and Rita jumped in the back, and Tim rattled off down the road. "What's the number six for?" I asked him, trying to break the mood.

Tim laughed. "Oh, I call her Sixball," he said, slapping the dashboard, " 'cause she's the same color as a six ball. Somebody painted the sixes on the doors one night while I was playing pool in the Saddlerack. I never did find out who did it. Everyone knows I call her that."

Another prank, I thought, but a playful one this time. At the moment, I'd had enough of pranks, of any kind. That was the trouble with these little, tiny communities. Everyone knew everyone else, and in these quiet towns there wasn't a lot to do but mind your neighbors' business. It was the main form of entertainment. And it sometimes made for a lot of trouble and unpleasant gossip. But stalking?

Tim passed the big house, which sat quiet in the morning sunshine. Joyce's midnight blue Cadillac was parked in the driveway. Glen's truck was nowhere in sight. Tim kept going.

Then we were down the hill and the barnyard and roping arena were ahead. We could all see Glen, saddling Smoke, who was tied to the hitching rail. Everything seemed normal. I could feel Lisa let out a small sigh next to me.

Business was as usual at the Bennett Ranch. Forgetting my worries, I regarded the cluster of old buildings and corrals with pleasure. The barnyard, like Lisa's house, dated from the ranch's early days; the two big old barns, much repaired, were high-roofed and cavernous, their siding weathered to a silvery gray. A couple of small sheds and other outbuildings and a good many corrals clustered around them.

All the buildings bore the names of their original purpose. Thus the biggest barn was still called the dairy barn, though the dairy cattle were long gone; the second largest was the hay barn; the smaller buildings the calf shed, milk house, bull barn, respectively. Glen had altered them just enough to use them comfortably as a horse setup, but they still had the look and character of the turn-of-the-century dairy they had been. It was part of what I had always loved about the place.

Tim parked Sixball, and the three of us got out of the truck. "Morning, Glen," I said.

He looked up from tightening the cinch and smiled at me, the old, familiar Glen Bennett smile, a flash of white teeth and blue eyes, an instant of warmth and charm. I was immediately transported back to a sixteen-year-old who had been half-infatuated with Lisa's handsome father.

"Well, hello, Gail. Did you come to help us gather?"

"I sure did."

"She's going to ride Chester," Lisa said. "He's for sale," she added to me. "If you know anyone who wants a nice young horse."

She got Chester out of his pen, and I looked the colt over. He was light-boned for a rope horse, but everything was in proportion and he had the sort of flat muscling I liked. He was about fifteen-two hands, and Lisa said he was five years old. Glen wanted $6,000 for him.

"He's ready to campaign at the heels," Lisa told me. "And he's real good outside—got a good handle on him, watches a cow real well. You'll see." She was saddling the horse as she spoke and handed his reins to me when she was done.

"He's not cinchy or anything, is he?" I asked cautiously. The last thing I needed was to be bucked off.

"Chester? No way. He's never humped his back in his life. He's dead gentle."

Good. I climbed on and walked the colt around a little, getting the feel of him. Tim was saddling the roan mare he'd ridden yesterday, and Lisa got another blue roan mare who looked exactly like Smoke out of her stall.

"Did you raise all these?" I asked Glen, who had mounted his stallion and sat waiting.

"They're all by him," he said, looking down at Smoke. "And out of that good bay mare I used to rope on. Remember her? Annie Oakley was her name."

"Oh, yeah, Annie." I did remember. Annie was the horse Glen had roped on when I was young. "Is she still alive?"

"She's almost thirty," he said proudly, "but she still has a foal every year. She just foaled two days ago." He waved a hand at a small field off to the side of the barn.

I looked where he pointed and saw a bay mare I recognized as Annie. Her back was deeply swayed and there were hollows over her eyes and a lot of gray hairs in her forehead, but she looked healthy and in good flesh. Next to her stood a bay foal.

He was tiny and new and perfect, long-legged and bright-eyed, with a high curved neck like a seahorse. I smiled in delight at the sight of him.

"He's a clone of Chester," Lisa said. "I think he'll be a good one."

"These three," Glen indicated the two roan mares and Chester, "are all full brothers and sisters to him."

"That's Roany," Lisa said, pointing at the big mare Tim was sitting on. "She's the oldest. She's six. And this is Rosie." She patted the neck of the mare she was saddling. "She's four. We lost their three-year-old full brother just a month ago."

Silence followed that remark. I remembered Lisa telling me that Glen had lost his three-year-old when the colt had gotten into the gopher grain. Another accident.

I patted Chester's neck. How could anybody do that? Could anybody really do that? Surely not Tim.

Tim sat quietly on Roany, not taking part in the conversation. He held himself stiffly, for Tim, and it was easy to imagine that he hurt all over. Glen had not said one word about the condition of his son's face; in fact, he wouldn't look at Tim. What in the hell was going on here?

Lisa climbed on Rosie and Glen lifted his reins. "Let's go find 'em," he said.

ELEVEN

We started down a dirt road that led into the hills of the home pasture. Dust rose under the horses' hooves. The dogs trotted behind us. It was already hot. Pretty damn hot for May, or so I thought. I was sweating in a matter of minutes. So was Chester.

I could smell the dusty dry-grass smell, a midsummer smell. The grass was bleached gold on this south slope, and sparse at that. "Not much feed left," I said to Glen.

"It's all gone," he agreed. "Been a bad year. The cattle have done all right so far, but I'll have to ship them now. There's nothing left for them to eat. I doubt I'll make any money on them. Any other year, I would have had another month for sure." Glen didn't sound particularly concerned. Money wasn't a worry for him, as far as I knew.

Chester walked along under me, quiet and relaxed. He was proving to be a pleasant, responsive horse to ride, with a light mouth and a long, swinging walk that covered the ground. I liked him.

I ran my eyes over the empty gold hills, looking for cattle. None in sight. I could hear quail in the brush. A little breeze rippled the grass, brushing it backward with a flash of silver. The sky was an even, hot, cloudless blue. And suddenly, without warning, I felt an intense longing for Lonny.

Normally I would have called him, we'd have come up together with our own horses, he'd be riding next to me now on Burt. Lonny would like nothing better than to help Glen gather cattle on a sunny morning. We would smile at each other, sharing our pleasure in the horses, the empty hills, the day.

Pain, like a rush of blood, poured through me. Maybe Lonny had spent the night with Sara. Maybe Lonny and I were over.

I tried to shut my mind to the feelings. Looked down at Chester, felt of his smooth walk, brushed a strand of his black mane back on the right side of his neck.

I wanted to go back in time. Less than six months ago, Lonny and I had been solidly together, had been happy. Now everything had changed. I wanted to break the unreasonable law that had dragged me to the present state of affairs. I wanted it to be last year again, when Sara lived with her doctor and Lonny still loved me.

Lonny, Lonny, Lonny. Chester's hooves seemed to tap it out. Lisa and Glen and Tim rode in silence. Except for the occasional circling hawk above, we were the only living things in sight. The quiet seemed to stretch out, reaching up to the sky. The hooves clopped softly in the dirt; saddles squeaked; bits and spurs jingled. Chester snorted softly.

Slowly Lonny seeped back out of my mind. For right now it was these empty hills, these horses, this last remnant of the Old West. I reached down to pat Chester's neck. I'd be OK, I told myself. I'd be OK.

We rode down a gully. The road made a turn and there was an old concrete water trough with some thirty steers around it. The cattle stared at us, heads raised in mild alarm. They were Brahma-cross cattle, leggy, with long ears and an alert, wild look, different in some essential, basic way from the quiet, short-legged, round-headed Herefords and black baldies Glen had kept when I was young. These cattle had, in their dark eyes, some of the force and power of wild animals. We stood there quietly, watching them.

"They look pretty good," I said to Glen.

He nodded. "These crossbred cattle do well in this country."

Lisa's blue dog trotted up to the water trough, put his front paws on the rim, and jumped in. It was a deep trough, and he disappeared completely, with a splash. It didn't seem to disconcert him. His head bobbed up, wet and sleek as a seal, and he swam around a minute before putting his paws on the edge and dragging himself ungracefully out. He shook the water from his coat happily, as the cattle watched him with suspicion.

"They're sixty steers in this field," Glen said. "About half of them are here. I think the rest will be up this canyon." He waved an arm off to the right. "Tim and I will go up there. Lisa, why don't you and Gail ride up to the back side in case there're a few at the water hole. We'll pick this group up on the way back."

"OK." Lisa turned her mare and I followed. The two dogs went with us.

We rode along the side of the gully for a while. I peered into the shadows under the oak trees, looking for the shapes or the movement of cattle. I didn't see anything.

The gully began to peter out. It headed more and more steeply uphill, got shallower and shallower. In places it was little more than a ditch. There were no more trees. The sun beat relentlessly down. Chester's neck was wet with sweat; the dogs trotted in our shadows, tongues hanging out, panting steadily. If I remembered right, we were nearing the back of the pasture.

We rode up a short, steep rise, Chester scrambling a little, and stood on the rim of a small basin. Ten steers were gathered around the pond in the bottom. It was just a hollow right near the ridgeline, bare and treeless. I could see the back fence of the pasture on the ridge beyond.

Lisa and I stared down at the steers. They stared up at us, looking ready to run at the slightest encouragement.

"This is all that we'll find back here," Lisa said softly. "If they're not at this water hole, they won't be up here."

"So, what do you want to do?"

"Sneak around 'em. Get 'em headed downhill. At a walk, if we can. They'll follow the gully back to where we saw the other cattle. The main problem is not letting any get off in the brush. These Brahma cattle are pretty wiley. We need to keep them in sight."

Lisa turned her mare and began to walk quietly around the basin, meaning to ease the cattle off in the direction we had come from. I followed her, keeping my head turned away from the cattle, as if I weren't interested in them. Eye contact alone can start a spooky steer into a run.

I'd only taken a few steps when I saw two small blurred streaks out of the corner of my eye. I jerked my head around in time to see Joey and Rita barrel into the middle of the steers, full tilt, snapping at heels and noses indiscriminately. There was a second of confused dust and motion, a bawl from a startled steer, and then the cattle vanished over the rim of the hollow, heads and tails up, going downhill at a dead run.

"Dammit!" Lisa yelled at the top of her voice. She also yelled, "Come back here!," but she didn't waste any time waiting for the dogs to obey. She yelled as she started Rosie down the hill at a gallop, following the cloud of dust that was the cattle. I gave Chester his head and clucked to him.

Hills and sky seemed to blend in a rushing blue. Chester scrambled beneath me on the steep ground, clever as a cat, keeping his footing easily, even while running downhill. I tried to stay balanced and in the middle of him, my weight back, focusing on guiding him around rocks, holes, and major obstacles. I let him take care of the minor ones.

I could see Lisa and the cattle ahead of us. Hot wind whipped my face as I felt the horse grunting, the sudden shift and roll of his body. Going hard in a flat place, keeping the cattle in sight, checking down for a steep spot, a sliding, slithering trot, then back at the run where the ground leveled out. I felt drunk on the wind and the rhythm of the chase. If Chester went down and killed me now, I wouldn't care. I clucked to him and leaned forward and felt him stretch out a little harder.

It had taken us half an hour to ride up the gully; it took us about ten minutes to come back down it. Chester was gasping for air as we neared the water trough. Even the long-legged Brahma steers were loping, rather than running, looking for a place to stop. The dogs loped behind them, tongues almost touching the ground.

"Joey, Rita, come here," Lisa ordered, pulling her mare up.

They looked over their shoulders, appeared to consider the matter, and then trotted wearily back in our direction. They sat down next to Lisa's horse and looked up at her. "Good dogs," she said.

The cattle broke into a walk immediately. We trailed after them in a leisurely fashion until they met up with the group around the water trough. They all milled a little, but they looked like they were planning to stay put. Tim and Glen weren't around. Lisa and I parked our horses under a shade tree. I patted Chester's wet neck. "You're a good boy," I told him. "I'll ride you on a gather any old day."

Five minutes later, Glen appeared, pushing another twenty or so steers. Glen counted heads and announced we had everything. We began trailing them down the dirt road toward the corrals. "Where's Tim?" I asked.

"He went on home," Glen said. "Said he wasn't feeling well."

I could guess why.

Lisa gave me a crooked smile. "A little dusty, huh?" She seemed relaxed and happy, despite the cloud of dirt that was billowing around us, filling our eyes and noses and coating our hair.

We got the cattle in the corral without any trouble. They were tired. Both Joey and Rita jumped in the water trough and swam around. I unsaddled Chester. Glen got beers out of the refrigerator in the barn and passed them around. I took a long, cold swallow. Nothing, I thought, tasted better than ice-cold beer when you were hot and tired and dusty.

I had Chester hosed and scraped and was almost done with my beer when Lisa came running around the corner of the barn, her eyes wide and frantic. "The colt!" she almost screamed. "The colt!"

Her fear seemed unmanageable, her eyes blank with terror.

"What's wrong?" I demanded.

Lisa's voice was shaking. "The colt's dead," she said. "Someone cut his throat."

TWELVE

The foal lay on the ground, flat on his side, a few feet from the wall of the barn. From a distance he appeared merely asleep. But the old mare stood over him, nosing him and nickering anxiously. Clenching my jaw, I approached his carcass.

There was a small pool of blood on the ground next to him; most of it had already soaked into the dust, leaving only a dark stain. Flies buzzed greedily over what was left. I stared at the jagged tear in his neck, then bent down and examined it closely.

After a minute I stood and met Glen's eyes. "He bled to death," I said evenly. "His jugular vein is torn open."

I stared down at the little corpse, which only a few hours ago had been a living baby horse—a minor miracle. Now he was dead. An accident?

As if reading my mind, Glen said, "He must have gotten cut on a nail or something." Turning, he began to examine the barn wall nearest to where the colt lay. In a minute he pointed at a large nail that was sticking out of a split board. "Like this," he said. "Goddamn old buildings."

I walked over and looked at the nail. Maybe, I thought, maybe. I'd seen horses hurt themselves this badly on sticks and broken boards and the insignificant-looking prongs of barbed wire. Only last week I'd been called out to treat a mare who had bled to death before I'd gotten there; she'd caught her foot in a barbed-wire fence and ripped an artery wide open.

Glen's voice brought me to myself. "Poor little guy," he said sadly. "I guess I better go get the tractor. It won't take much of a hole to bury him."

Lisa stood ten steps away, not looking at the colt, hugging herself with both arms. "This wasn't an accident," she said dully. "Somebody killed that colt."

Glen just shook his head. "I'll go get the tractor." He turned and walked away.

Lisa grabbed my arm. "Come on. I need to get out of here."

Without asking, she climbed into her father's truck; the two dogs jumped into the bed behind us. I stared out the passenger window at the double-wide mobile home that sat between the roping arena and the ranch entrance. Al Borba's residence. The curtains were all drawn closed. No way to know who was inside. But there was a brown pickup and a red Trans Am in the driveway.

To my surprise, Lisa drove out the ranch entrance rather than up the hill toward her house. "I'll buy you lunch," she said, feeling my eyes on her.

In another minute we were parked in front of the Saddlerack. I noted that I could see the roping arena from here and parts of the barnyard, though the field where the dead foal lay was hidden behind the barn. A person could easily have watched us saddling horses and departing to gather from this spot.

I followed Lisa into the cool, dim interior of the empty bar, and we sat down at the round table in the corner. A man was tending bar today—an older man with a battered face and a heavy, big-boned frame.

"Where's Janey?" I asked Lisa.

"She doesn't work Sundays," Lisa said absently. "Len does."

That brought another question to mind. "How come Al didn't help us gather this morning?"

"He doesn't work Sundays, either."

So Al, and for that matter Janey, had been free all morning. Free to kill colts, if that happened to be their inclination.

Lisa got up and ordered beer and hamburgers from the bartender. She brought the beer back to our table. "Len'll bring the hamburgers out here," she said.

I took a long swallow of beer, feeling as though I were washing the taste of blood out of my mouth.

"So, what do you think, Gail?" Lisa demanded.

"I think you're right. I think there've been too many accidents."

"You think someone killed that colt?"

"It's possible," I said slowly. "That wound could have been made by a knife. And there wasn't any blood on the nail Glen showed me. But we can't prove it. And why would anybody kill that baby?"

"Because he belonged to Dad," Lisa retorted. "Because Dad was proud of him. There's no other reason."

"That's scary."

"I know it's scary. That's what I've been telling you. Gail, we've got to figure out who's doing these things."

"I tend to agree with you. I just don't know how to do it. I can hardly ask your friend the bartender if he noticed anybody driving into the ranch this morning. That would start just the sort of talk Glen wants to avoid."

"I know," Lisa agreed miserably. "But I don't care anymore who talks about what. I just want to catch the bastard who's doing this. That poor little foal." Lisa sounded ready to burst into tears.

"How could anybody do that?" I said, mostly to myself. "Of course, it could have been an accident. It was an irregular tear, not a nice neat cut." What I was thinking but didn't say was that

I wished like hell Tim hadn't gone home ahead of us. Roany had been in her pen when we got to the barn. Had Tim put her up and left, never noticing that the foal was dead? It was more than possible. To a casual glance, the foal would have looked asleep, sacked out on his side. Foals often slept that way.

Or had someone killed the foal in the window of time between Tim's return to the barn and our own? It seemed unlikely. Or, worst-case scenario, had Tim killed the foal? He was the one person known to have been there at the right time. But these weren't things I wanted to say to Lisa. The thought of Tim cutting the foal's throat was so bizarre as to be terrifying.

The bartender brought our hamburgers, and both of us dug in. Despite the tragedy of the foal and my worries about Lonny, I found I was ravenous. Riding a horse all morning will do that for you. Lisa and I finished the burgers, and Lisa reached for the check and stuck a hand in the pocket of her jeans. "Damn," she said and got up from the table. "Dad'll have some money in the truck."

"I'll get it," I offered.

"No, you helped us this morning. We're buying your lunch. I'll be right back."

Lisa disappeared out the door, and I took a last, long swallow of beer. What now? I asked myself. Call the cops, my mind answered. To hell with the talk. This is dangerous stuff. Someone really hates Glen.

But what could the cops do? No one had been hurt or killed. No people, anyway. Cops weren't interested in dead horses. Particularly when we couldn't prove that the deaths hadn't all been accidents.

Call a private detective? I was trying to decide if this was a possibility when all hell broke loose outside the bar. Dogs barking and snarling, a man yelling, and Lisa's voice raised in alarm. I almost tipped the table over in my rush out the door.

It took me a minute to sort out the scene in the parking lot, which looked like a small-scale war. Lisa was standing by the pickup. In front of her, yelling and cussing, was a tall, dark man in a cowboy hat. It was Sonny, all right. But he wasn't yelling at Lisa. Dive-bombing him, barking and snarling, were the two Queenslands. They were making so much noise they were drowning Sonny out, and he was shouting at the top of his lungs. Judging by the expression on his face, some of the strikes were connecting.

I came to a dead stop. The bartender almost ran into my backside; he'd come charging out of the bar right on my heels. He looked at me, a wide grin spreading across his face. I could feel a similar smile breaking out on my own. The sight of Sonny Santos being attacked by his own dogs was pretty funny.

Sonny was losing the battle. He would aim a savage kick at one dog and, as it would duck out of the way, the other dog would come in and bite him. Most of the bites were landing on his calves; the dogs seemed smart enough to grab over the tops of his cowboy boots. Once in a while one of his kicks would land firmly and a dog would yelp, but they weren't quitting. Queenslands aren't bred to quit. They snarled and dove back in on him.

Between the dust and noise and commotion, Sonny didn't even notice Len and me. It only took a minute before he realized the dogs wouldn't quit and Lisa wasn't going to call them off. He struggled back to his pickup, fighting a rearguard action. Even so, he got bitten a few more times. His cussing was getting angrier and more obscene, but there wasn't much he could do. He managed to get in the pickup and shut the door.

Lisa was standing next to me by this time. She called the dogs to her and looked at me with sudden fear in her eyes. "What if he has a gun?"

I'd wondered that myself. Lisa had the Queenslands by their collars, keeping them next to her. I watched Sonny carefully to see what he'd do next.

The bartender watched him with a wide grin. I had a sense Len was hoping for trouble. After a minute, I was pretty sure

Sonny didn't have a gun. The anger on his face was murderous. If he'd had a gun, he would have produced it.

He leaned his head out the window. All his rage was focused on Lisa, who stood next to me, holding the dogs.

"You little bitch," he yelled. "I'm not done with you yet!"

To my surprise, Lisa yelled back. "Knock it off, Sonny. I'm done with you. And if you ever set foot on the ranch I'm calling the cops!"

Sonny looked mad enough to burst a blood vessel. All his cool arrogance had vanished in the heat of battling his own dogs. His face was flushed and red.

"You'll be sorry, you bitch," he shouted. Then he threw the truck into gear and accelerated out of the parking lot in a cloud of dust, barely missing Glen's pickup.

Lisa gave me an intense look. "We better get back to the ranch. Who knows what he'll do?"

"All right," I agreed.

Lisa paid Len for our lunches, ignoring his amused smile, and we headed back toward her place. I kept my eyes open as we drove in. Al's mobile home was still quiet and shuttered; the same two vehicles were parked beside it. A green tractor sat next to the barn where it hadn't been before, but Glen was nowhere in sight. Tim's truck and Joyce's Cadillac sat in the driveway of the big house. I didn't see any unexpected visitors or any cars or trucks that didn't belong. In front of Lisa's house was just my own truck with the veterinary cabinets on the back—friendly and familiar.

At the sight of it, I was suddenly ready to go. I'd had enough of the Bennett Ranch. Resisting Lisa's pleas, I told her I needed to get home. Had to meet my realtor, I added, a palpable lie. The truth was I wanted out of this alarming soap opera. My own life, however grim it was at the moment, seemed wonderfully restful in comparison.

All the way down Lone Oak Road, though, I couldn't keep my mind off Lisa's stalker. This shadowy figure who had killed three horses already was assuming an ever-more-ominous presence. I couldn't tell myself that Lisa was imagining things—not after seeing the dead foal. I knew that in my heart I didn't really believe that colt had died by accident.

When I pulled in my driveway half an hour later, I hadn't come any closer to a solution. I stormed in the house feeling frustrated and half-scared. A note from Denise said she'd shown the place to two more people and the schoolteacher had called back. She'd be in touch, Denise had added.

I played the answering machine tape. Only one message, but it was from Lonny. At the sound of his familiar voice, my heart jumped in my chest.

"Gail, come over this evening. I'll cook you dinner. If I don't hear from you, I'll assume you'll be here." Click.

Now what? I glanced at the clock. It was only three. Well, the first thing was to get cleaned up.

An hour later I'd showered, shaved my legs, blow-dried my hair, and applied the blush and lip gloss that was all the makeup I used. I stood in front of my closet, staring at the rack of clothes, trying to decide what to wear.

Now was the time, I thought a little sadly, for something revealing and sexy, if I had any such thing. I was a solid fourteen years younger than Sara. I ought to make the most of it.

Trouble was, I'd never gone in for glamorous dressing. I'm just not the glamorous type. Something in the very features of my face says casual. On top of which, I told myself, I was damned if I was going to try and lure Lonny back into a relationship. We'd been together almost four years. He knew who I was. If he didn't want to put out for me, it was better to let him go.

Brave words. I still wanted to look good. I studied the row of clothes in my closet, a muted harmony of greens, tans, browns, and blues. Lately I'd developed a liking for these quiet colors—the vivid violets, turquoises, and watermelon pinks I'd chosen for years suddenly seemed garish. I was getting older, maybe.

95

After a minute I gave up the search. There was nothing in here I hadn't seen before. I pulled on a pair of chino shorts and my favorite silk blouse—a soft sage green. Woven leather flats on my feet, freshwater pearls around my neck, and my rambunctious hair brushed into the closest semblance to soft waves I could manage, and I was done.

Turning my face firmly away from the mirror, I climbed my ladder stairway and looked at the clock. Only four. Pretty early for dinner.

Of course, any time but lately, I would have dropped in on Lonny whenever I felt like it, certain I'd be welcome. But now I was afraid to.

Shit. Damn Sara, anyway. She hovered in the background of my life, a shadowy bogeyman. The all-powerful Wicked Witch of the West. Just like Lisa's stalker, I thought suddenly.

I looked at the clock again. I was tired of feeling frustrated and impotent. I needed to do something positive, make something happen.

Well, there was one thing, I thought. Suddenly resolved, I headed out to the truck. I was going to meet Sara.

THIRTEEN

I knew where Sara lived; I'd seen the address on the checks Lonny sent her. West Cliff Drive, in Santa Cruz. It only took me twenty minutes to get there.

I parked outside the apartment building and looked up at it. A square, ugly block of concrete, the place featured a dramatic view of the bay, with Lighthouse Point in the foreground. It was, no doubt, pricey and probably carried prestige of a sort, but I thought the boring green lawns surrounding the gray-walled terraces and balconies all added up to a depressing total. No imagination and too much proximity to other human beings. Not my choice of a good way to live.

Now that I was here, I was having trouble getting out of the truck. My heart was beating hard, my hands were sweating, and I felt tight all over. Maybe this wasn't such a good idea. I had no clue what I would say to Sara, and every bit of ingenuity I possessed seemed to slip away from me with the prospect of a confrontation ahead.

What the hell. I got out of the truck normally, not slow, not fast, as though this was an ordinary visit, as though Sara and I were friends. I locked the truck. Put the keys in my pocket.

Walked toward the complex, looking for number 207. A quick evaluation put it upstairs, on the second story.

I climbed the black metal stairway. The view was something from up here. I could see all the way to Monterey, a low ridge of blue hills on the other side of the bay. Even on this hot afternoon, a cool breeze riffled off the water, smelling gently of seaweed and brine. I was at the door. I knocked.

My heart thudded steadily. What should I say? "Hello," I supposed, but then what? Maybe I could pretend to be a salesman.

For a minute my knock went unanswered and I felt a surge of relief at the idea she wasn't home. Then the door opened a few inches, still on the chain. "Yes?" she said.

So this was Sara. She would be almost fifty, I knew, but she looked much younger. Smooth, shiny light brown hair, free of any tint of gray, just touched her shoulders. She wore white shorts and a pale blue linen blouse, and the shorts revealed slim legs with a good tan. She was a full head shorter than me, probably about five-two, and delicately made, with small bones. The big dark blue eyes with fine brows were carefully and expertly made up. She looked fragile, clean, perfect—like a doll in a china hutch.

I took all this in in a long second of staring through the four-inch crack between the door and the jamb, all my senses on ultra-alert. I was certain I could smell her perfume, light and lemony. I still hadn't said a word.

Recognition dawned slowly on her face. For whatever reason, however it had come about, she knew who I was. Maybe she had seen me with Lonny. She spoke slowly. "You're Gail, aren't you?"

I nodded mutely.

"Lonny's girlfriend." Her tone had gone from confused to unfriendly.

I still didn't know what to say. I felt like some dumb, begging animal, here at her door, expecting something, I wasn't sure what. She wasn't going to pat me on the head and say I was welcome to her husband.

"I wanted to meet you," I got out.

She didn't take the chain off the door, just continued regarding me through the crack. She looked annoyed, doubtful, and a little nervous, all at once. Suddenly, I didn't blame her. She probably thought I was here to shoot her.

I stretched my hands out at my sides, so she could see they were empty. "Really. I just wanted to meet you. That's all."

"Lonny's my husband," she said at last. "I want you to leave him alone."

"You left him," I protested. "Years ago. You only want him back because your boyfriend left you." Now I sounded spiteful.

It made her mad. "Get out of here," she said harshly. "You've got no business coming between a man and his wife. I'm calling the police if you don't leave right now." And she slammed the door. I could hear the dead bolt shooting home.

For a second I stared at the shiny gray-painted surface. Damn. That was Sara. The woman Lonny had been married to. Was still married to. I couldn't quite take it in. She looked so different from what I'd expected, though I wasn't really sure what my expectations had added up to. Someone older-looking, less put-together and poised.

Still, I found her distinctly unappealing. Not just because she was Lonny's wife, I told myself. She was too clean, too precise, every hair in place. I supposed the shrinks called it anal retentive. Whatever it was, it was a demeanor I'd run into before, and it was never associated with an easygoing personality. With a slight sense of shock, I realized that Sara reminded me of Joyce Bennett.

Well, Lonny and Glen had a certain number of similarities. They were near the same age, though Lonny was a good five years younger than Glen, I reassured myself. But still, it made me feel odd. The man who had chosen this woman had later chosen me. I hoped I didn't have too much in common with Sara and Joyce.

Belatedly I realized I'd better get the hell out of here if I didn't want Lonny's wife calling the cops on me. I started down the steps, my heart growing lighter with every stride. It had worked, I thought. I was no longer so afraid of Sara.

She was just another human being, with unexpected faults and strengths; she wasn't some omnipotent, mythical, all-powerful wife figure. I could see her as a person, recognize that to her I was her husband's slutty younger girlfriend. I almost laughed out loud at the thought of her wondering to herself what he saw in me.

Climbing back in my truck, I drove off, relieved, for the moment, of the heavy weight I'd been carrying for months now. I could practically find it in me to feel sorry for Sara.

Almost but not quite. As I pointed the truck toward Lonny's, I took rapid stock of the situation. Despite the relief I felt, the question remained the same. Sara had made it clear what she wanted. Was Lonny going to let her move back in with him or not?

At the thought, my high spirits died a sudden death. I made the rest of the trip out to Lonny's in somber contemplation of my options. That is, if I had any. Maybe Lonny and Sara had come to an agreement last night.

When I turned in Lonny's driveway, I parked my truck at the barn, rather than driving up the hill to the house. I need to visit my horses, I told myself. But I was aware that I was reluctant to face Lonny.

Gunner and Plumber lifted their heads and nickered at me as I walked toward their pen. It was obvious Lonny had just fed them dinner; everybody was eating. Burt and Pistol nickered softly, too, and I stopped to look at Pistol. He was putting some weight on his right front leg, at least.

I leaned on the fence for a while, rubbing my two geldings on their foreheads, watching them eat. Putting off the inevitable. Gunner stretched his nose out to my face, and I blew into his nostrils, greeting him the way horses greet each other. Plumber was shyer; I stroked his cocoa-colored shoulder, telling him what a good horse he was and that I'd be riding him soon. Eventually, though, I gave each of them a final pat and turned away.

No point in standing here until they entirely ruined my silk blouse. I had to face the music sometime. Might as well be now.

I pulled up to Lonny's house in a regular froth of anxiety; I felt almost as nervous as when I'd gone to Sara's. This is stupid, I told myself firmly. After four years, almost, you shouldn't have to feel like this.

But I did. I was afraid. Afraid Lonny was going back to Sara. Afraid we were over. Afraid that this house, once so familiar, was open to me no longer.

The house looked as welcoming as ever on this warm spring evening. It was a round house, a decagon, surrounded by oak trees, with a cupola on top. Off to one side was a bricked-in kitchen garden, and on the other side tall windows were open to the breezes that drifted through the oak grove. I walked slowly to the front door, which was standing ajar.

Lonny was in the kitchen, pouring some kind of marinade over what looked like chicken. My favorite sauvignon blanc was in a bottle of ice on the counter next to him. He continued fussing with the meat, unaware of my presence.

He's getting deaf, I thought vaguely. He was fifty. No longer young. What do you want with an old man? I asked myself.

Lonny looked up, saw me, and smiled. Instantly his somewhat homely face was transformed, the vitality of his enthusiasm and warmth making him appear much younger.

"Hi," I said.

"Hello, love," he said. "Care for a glass of wine?"

"I guess so." I took the glass he offered me and sat down at the kitchen table. The top half of the Dutch door that led out into the little garden was open, and I could see onto the brick patio, with salmon-colored climbing roses draping the low walls, rows of neat young vegetable plants in a plot off to the side.

It was one of the things I liked about Lonny—the way he tended this house and garden. Everything, from the color of the mounded lavender-blue cranesbill geraniums that clustered at the feet of the roses to the finish on the terra-cotta tile floor in the living room, was carefully and lovingly detailed. Lonny took good care of what he valued, and he valued this property—a big reason, I knew, that a divorce would be terribly hard for him.

"How was your dinner with Sara?" I asked, wanting to get it over with.

"Tense. She wants me to go to counseling with her. Wants to try and save our marriage." Lonny's voice was very steady and even—deliberately so, I guessed.

"What did you tell her?"

"I said I'd think about it."

"What are you going to do?"

"I don't know. Think about it, I guess." Lonny poured himself a glass of wine and sat down next to me.

"What about us?" I asked him.

"Gail, I think that's up to you." He hesitated. "Would you marry me?"

I almost dropped my glass of wine. "Marry you? What are you talking about? You're married. I can't marry you."

"If I were to get divorced," Lonny said quietly, "would you marry me?"

"Are you proposing?"

"Sort of."

I laughed. "Let me get this straight. You're trying to find out if I'll marry you, if you get divorced. Sort of a bird-in-the-hand-is-worth-two-in-the-bush approach. You don't want to be left in the lurch."

"More or less."

I took a swallow of wine. "I don't think that's the best way to do this, Lonny. I don't want you to marry me because you don't want to be alone."

102

Lonny stared down at the wine in his glass. "Gail, I'm fifty. I'm too old to want to start over from scratch. If I divorce Sara, I'll end up selling almost everything I own. This place will go for sure. I know you're in the process of selling your house. I thought if we got married we could buy a place together, have a life, if you see what I mean."

I saw. It did have some appeal. Before I could speak, Lonny went on, "I've been thinking that I'd like to move up to the Sierra foothills, maybe around Mariposa. Land's a lot cheaper up there. We could afford to buy a ranch, not just a few acres."

I looked at him in disbelief. "You want me to marry you, quit my job, and leave my hometown, all at once? That's a lot to ask."

"Not really. Lots of women did it in the old days."

"Well, it's not the old days." Despite the fact that I was touched and reassured by Lonny's offer, I wasn't entirely pleased. I could not picture throwing away the independent life I'd built so carefully. Not for anybody. Striving to turn the subject, I said, "I think you need to make up your mind about getting the divorce, first."

Lonny sighed. "I suppose you're right." He got up and carried the marinated chicken out on the patio, where a curl of smoke rose from the coals in the barbecue pit. I followed him and sat down at the table by the flower bed. Bees buzzed on a clump of geraniums; a hummingbird swooped down to sip from a blue spike of larkspur.

"How do you feel about Sara?" I asked after a while.

"Mixed up." Lonny was watching the meat sputter. "Sorry for her some, like I'm partly to blame for the state she's in; pissed off at her a little, for being so difficult."

"Do you want to be with her again?"

Lonny looked at me in surprise. "Hell no. I want to be with you. I just don't want to deal with all this strife and financial havoc."

I couldn't really blame him. "If you did get the divorce," I said carefully, "is there any reason we couldn't go back to the way we were?"

"You mean living separately but being a couple?"

"Yeah. What's wrong with being independent and monogamous?"

"Nothing, I guess. Except I think I'd like to live with you."

I reached for his free hand and held it. "Lonny, I can be a pain. You know that. I'm prickly as hell a lot of the time. I need my space."

Lonny squeezed my hand and let it go. He started taking the meat off the grill. "I was afraid you'd say that," he said quietly. "Come on. Let's have dinner."

We ate salad and chicken and garlic bread, washed down by the excellent white wine. Lonny's two cats, Sam and Gandalf, sat on the table and watched every bite that moved from the plate to our mouths. I did not allow Bonner to do this at my house. But this was Lonny's house and these were his cats. I was used to them begging. One more reason, I thought idly, to have my own place. It was a lot easier to be tolerant.

When dinner was over, Lonny made coffee and we sat down on the Navajo-patterned couch in his living room. Mostly to keep the conversation away from "us," I told him about the problems at the Bennett Ranch. Lonny had known Glen for many years. Maybe he could provide an insight.

"So who might hate Glen Bennett enough to stalk him like that?" I asked.

"I wouldn't know, if it wasn't his wife."

"Joyce? You think Joyce hates Glen?"

Lonny shook his head. "That Joyce is a first-class bitch."

"I don't much like Joyce either, but why do you say that?"

Lonny twitched one shoulder. "Glen's first wife, those kids' mother, was a real nice woman. Marie, her name was. When she died, it tore Glen up something terrible. He was in a daze for months. Joyce got her hooks into him then. She was as sweet as sugar to him. It was 'Oh, Glen' this, and 'Oh, Glen' that. She wanted his money, or so we all thought. He couldn't see it. He was trying to raise those two tiny kids by himself, and I think he was as miserable as a man ever gets. To make a long story short, he married her within a year."

"I take it you didn't approve."

"Gail, Joyce has made Glen's life hell for years. She spends his money like it was water, nags him day and night, and runs around like the dirty whore she is."

I nodded. None of this was entirely news. I had seen a few of Joyce's tantrums, and I'd heard rumors circulating about her before. "Of course, Glen's got Pat," I said.

"I wouldn't know about that." Lonny was curt. Talking about Joyce was one thing, it seemed, but talking about Glen's indiscretions was another. I wondered if it was just good-old-boys loyalty or if Lonny actually did know something about Glen and Pat.

"There's been talk about them forever," I prodded.

"Talk's cheap." Lonny was done gossiping. He got up off the couch and looked down at me. "Speaking of which, I've about had enough of it for one night. Are you ready to go to bed?"

I stared up at him, meeting the intensity of his green eyes. Lying with him would feel wonderful, but then what? Everything seemed to be in turmoil.

I stood. "Lonny," I said cautiously, "I don't think I'd better. I think I need to know what you decide about Sara. If you're going to work on your marriage, it would be easier if I had some distance from you. I don't want to feel too vulnerable."

"And if I decide to get divorced?"

"Then we'll talk about it."

"So you won't promise anything." Lonny's face looked old and sad.

I put my arms around him and hugged him. With my own face buried in his chest, I said, "I can't. I just can't. I've spent my whole life building this career. It's all I've got. Except you. And at this point, I don't even know if I've got you. You might go back to Sara. How can I make a commitment to you on those terms? If you get a divorce, I'll think about us getting married. Or at least living together. It's the best I can say."

Lonny put his arms around me, and we held each other for a moment. I could feel the solid warmth and comfort of his body, so dear and familiar. My life would seem pretty empty without him.

Abruptly I let go and headed for the door. "I'll see you tomorrow," I said. "Down at the clinic. We'll work on Pistol."

I went out before he could answer, got in my truck, started it, and drove out. All the way home there was only one issue on my mind: Lonny and what he wanted of me. Nothing less than giving up my life and my job for him. I wasn't sure I could do it. One thing I was sure of, though; if I'd slept with him tonight, I would have been sorely tempted to say yes.

FOURTEEN

At eight o'clock the next morning I was ready to ditch the job. I stood in the office of Santa Cruz Equine Practice, staring at the note that some kind soul had placed on my desk so I couldn't miss it. I said, "Oh, shit," out loud in a tone meant to carry.

Jim Leonard, my boss, sadistic bastard that he was, grinned at the words. "She asked for you, Gail. Not me. You."

I swiveled my gaze to the receptionist, who had been carefully avoiding my eye. "Is that true?"

"Uh, yeah, I'm afraid so. She said you were real good with Thunder last time. She thinks he likes you better than Jim."

"Great."

Jim's grin grew even wider. We were both quite familiar with Kelly Haynes and Thunder. Kelly wasn't so bad; her main fault was misguided loyalty to Thunder.

Thunder was purely an asshole. I thought myself he was also mentally retarded. Nothing else could entirely explain his colossal uncooperativeness and/or the stupidity expressed in violence that was his trademark. He frequently ended up injuring himself as well as the unfortunate humans who came in contact with him.

Thunder was known to flip over backward at the drop of a hat, both when being ridden and when being handled on the ground. At times it seemed he needed no reason; without the slightest warning he would fly backward, rear straight up, and go over, flattening anything behind him. He also bucked Kelly off whenever he felt like it, spooked violently at anything he didn't care for, was clumsy enough to have fallen with her several times, and bit and kicked when provoked. On top of which, he stood 16.2, weighed fourteen hundred pounds, and was as strong as those facts implied. Thunder had no redeeming qualities. He was one horse that belonged in a dog food can.

"So what's wrong with him now?" I asked the room at large.

"He's got an abscess, she thinks," the receptionist answered me.

"Wonderful."

Thunder couldn't stand having his feet worked on. Digging a sole abscess out of his hoof was bound to result in at least one back flip.

"I think I'm gonna need help with this." I turned to Jim, but he was already backing up.

"I've got a colic case out in Watsonville, Gail. An emergency. Got to go." A minute later, he was gone.

No help for it. I took my time organizing the things I needed and making sure my truck was well stocked, but eventually I had to head out. Working on difficult horses was part of my job; Jim would not forgive me for pleading cowardice.

The drive out to Kelly's was pleasant enough; I followed San Andreas Road along the cypress- and pine-tree-studded coastline, admiring the deep blue of Monterey Bay on this sunny May morning. Not a trace of fog was visible, and it was already warm at 9:00 A.M.; it was going to be another hot one.

I pulled into the white-board-fenced driveway and looked automatically at the corral next to the barn where Kelly kept

Thunder. There he was. He hadn't somehow managed to die before I got there. Damn.

Getting out of the truck reluctantly, I walked in his direction. Not a bad-looking horse, I thought idly. A shame he was so entirely worthless.

Half Quarter Horse, half Thoroughbred, Thunder was as well made as he was big. Many people had probably told Kelly what a good-looking horse he was. Too many. His bright red sorrel color, high white socks, big blaze, and flaxen mane and tail all added to the showy impression.

As I approached him, he pinned his ears and turned away, showing me his ass end and ruining his fancy appearance totally, as far as I was concerned. Such behavior was par for the course with Thunder; it wouldn't take an experienced horseman two minutes to figure out the horse was a bad one.

Kelly came walking out of her barn, carrying a halter. "Hi, Gail," she said. "Thanks for coming out. He's real lame in the left hind."

Shit. A hind foot. That was the kicking end.

"I think it's another abscess," she went on.

This was probably a good guess. In addition to his many other faults, Thunder had terrible feet. They were prone to cracking and chipping, they bruised easily, and they had a tendency to develop abscesses.

"Did he get real lame all of a sudden?" I asked Kelly.

"Yeah."

"Probably an abscess, then." Given Thunder's history, I was willing to bet on it, but, of course, I would have to examine him carefully first. Not a fun prospect.

Kelly went into the corral to catch the horse; despite the fact that he was quite dramatically lame in the left hind leg and was virtually hobbling, it took her ten minutes. Thunder was an expert on evasion.

Eventually she got him in a corner and was able to put the

halter on him. I approached warily. Being caught, with Thunder, was no guarantee that he would remain caught. He was very good at jerking the lead rope out of Kelly's hands. But tying him up was even more dangerous; it positively seemed to incite him to pull back.

Keeping my body well off to the side, I ran a hand down his left hind leg and picked the foot up. Thunder quivered, but he obliged, for the moment. I could feel no unnatural lumps or swellings on his leg; he had no obvious injuries. Now for the hard part.

Using a hoof knife, I cleaned the foot out and pared it down to clean, white sole. No nails or punctures or wedged pebbles were evident. I got the hoof testers and began the process of squeezing the sole in various spots, trying to find the sore place.

As I had more or less expected, Thunder reacted violently when I found it. Jerking his foot out of my hands, he reared up, dragging Kelly with him. I flung myself clear and waited. Thunder stood on his back legs and waved his front feet in the air for a minute, but eventually he came back down. Kelly managed to hang onto him. Not bad, for the first round.

"He's got an abscess," I told her. "Right in the heel. I'll need to block him and dig it out."

She nodded unhappily. She knew as well as I did what the abscess would entail. First the touchy process of opening it up so it could drain, then a weeklong regime of antibiotics, foot baths, and bandaging. Sole abscesses were a pain in the butt, particularly with an uncooperative horse like Thunder.

Getting some tranquilizer out of the truck, I gave Thunder a quick couple of cc's in the jugular vein, putting the shot in before he could really see what I was doing. Normally I wouldn't tranquilize a horse with a sole abscess—it makes it harder to hold up a foot—but with Thunder, I thought it would improve my odds of getting through doctoring him unscathed.

Once the horse was swaying slightly, I gave him a shot of nerve block in the ankle, to eliminate the pain my hoof knife would otherwise cause. Then I jacked his foot up on my knee, not without some effort, and began digging into him.

Thunder swayed, he leaned on me heavily, and he made several sharp attempts to jerk his foot away, but eventually I managed to cut deep enough to get the pus flowing. A few more good scrapes to make sure the abscess was fully opened and draining, and then I began bandaging the foot. It was when I was wrapping the duct tape over the gauze that I got in trouble.

Without any warning, or any hesitation, he kicked out, hard and fast. His lashing hoof missed my knee by a fraction of an inch, and I stumbled aside, just in time to get out of the way as he fired again. My muscles trembled, tried to their limits by the strain of holding up his leg for long minutes. Sweat soaked my shirt. I stood there, gasping for air, and watched the bastard leap around, destroying his half-finished bandage and filling his open wound with barnyard muck. It took all the self-control I possessed to keep my mouth shut.

I managed. I gave him another couple of cc's of tranquilizer and I cleaned and rewrapped his foot, more or less without incident. I accepted Kelly's thanks, handed her antibiotics, bandaging materials, and instructions, and made a reasonably graceful exit. Very professional. Inwardly, I was seething.

Calling the office from the car phone, with every intention of bawling Jim out and refusing to deal with Thunder ever again, I was slightly mollified by the receptionist's first words. "Gail, Kris Griffith called for you. Dixie has a cut on her poll that needs a couple of stitches."

This was good news. Dixie was a sweet-tempered mare, and Kris Griffith was a friend. "Call and tell her I'll be right there," I said.

Kris lived on Old San Jose Road, in the Soquel Valley, not too far from my little house. I'd boarded Gunner with her the first year I owned him, and I knew her place well. Driving in, I looked with familiar pleasure at the neat, corral-board-fenced pastures, the pretty barn, and the riding arena down by the creek. Kris's place was a horseman's paradise. Unfortunately, she was about to lose it.

Like everybody else, it seemed, Kris was in the process of a messy and unpleasant divorce, one that she'd put off for years, she told me, for financial reasons and out of fear of a custody battle. But things had eventually gotten bad enough she'd embarked on the struggle. Now her pretty ranch was up for sale and her daughter divided her time between mother and father. Why would anybody take the risk of getting married, I asked myself, not for the first time.

Pulling up to the barn, I looked automatically at Rebby's pen. There he was, an eleven-year-old dark brown gelding, a horse Kris had campaigned for many seasons at the top levels of endurance racing. A horse who had won the legendary Tevis Cup. And one of my worst veterinary failures. Rebby was crippled for life.

I got out of the truck and went over to pet him. Rubbing his forehead with its white star, I asked him, "So, how's Rebel Cause today?"

"The same," Kris said from behind me.

I turned to face her. Her tone was rueful but accepting; both she and I had had to come to terms with the fact that Rebby would never be sound again.

He had contracted EPM, a neurological condition that had left him with some permanent incoordination in his hind legs. I had treated him with the appropriate medication, but he had failed to make a complete recovery, whether because we hadn't started the treatment soon enough or just bad luck I didn't know. He wasn't in any pain, but he walked clumsily and occasionally fell when he tried to gallop. Kris had made the decision to keep him as a pet, and Rebby lived in a corral that was just big enough that he could move around and get some exercise and not so big he could run at breakneck speeds and kill himself.

It was difficult for everybody, not least of all for Reb. A strong-minded, athletic horse of mostly Thoroughbred descent,

Rebby had tons of go. Standing around in a pen was not his idea of a good time; traveling fifty miles on an outing was. But Kris had decided, wisely I thought, that it was too much of a risk to ride him; the potential for him to fall and kill them both was too great. So she took him for walks; she brushed him and petted him and cared for him and loved him. It was the best she could do. It was like having your child confined to a wheelchair for life: you cope.

Kris had never considered putting Rebby down. "This horse has done everything for me," she told me. "As long as he's not in pain, I'm not going to quit him."

And he wasn't. I looked into his dark, intelligent eyes as he bumped me with his nose, asking for more rubbing. The eyes were steady and kind and quiet; they sparkled with mischief at times. They were not the eyes of a horse in distress. I had always been quite sure that Reb's condition wasn't painful. Merely frustrating, as far as he was concerned.

"So, what happened to Dixie?" I asked Kris.

"She's got a cut on her poll. I think it needs a few stitches." Kris caught Dixie and led her out.

The little dun mare stood reasonably still as I scrutinized the wound between her ears but jerked her head up when I attempted to probe it. I didn't blame her. It probably hurt like hell.

"She must have thrown her head up and hit it on something sharp," I told Kris. "It might be deep. I'll have to tranquilize her so I can clean it. You might look around her corral for nails sticking out of boards and sharp branches."

"I'll do that." Kris watched me get the tranquilizer and inject it; in a minute the mare was swaying on her feet.

I cleaned and stitched Dixie's cut without incident; Kris gave me the particulars of her latest court battle with Rick while I worked. I didn't really want to hear it; I was reminded too much of what Lonny was dreading with Sara. But Kris was my friend, and I knew she needed to talk.

When the war stories and the stitching were both done, I asked her, "So what are you doing with this little horse?"

"Oh, I bought Dixie mostly for Jo." Kris's daughter had recently grown more interested in horses. "I take her on a trail ride once in a while; that's it."

"You don't plan to compete anymore?"

"No. Between working full-time and taking care of Jo and this damn divorce, I just don't have the energy; not to mention I'm mostly broke."

The horrors of the marital split. Lonny's fears were far from exaggerated. I wished Kris good luck, gave her antibiotics for Dixie, and told her to call me if she wanted to have lunch. Then I headed back to the clinic.

As I expected, Lonny was waiting for me. Pistol stood tied to the trailer, and Lonny sat in the patch of shade under the one tree in the office parking lot. When he saw me he got to his feet, a little haltingly, moving in that stiff way that let me know his arthritic hip was bothering him.

"Looks like I ought to give you some bute," I told him.

"You're not kidding." Lonny grinned. "Getting old is the pits."

He walked over to Pistol, untied him, and led him toward me. Immediately I could tell that the horse was no better. Dead lame in the right front.

"I took him off bute last night," Lonny said, "so we could see how he's doing."

"He doesn't look too good," I said. "I'm going to shoot some pictures of that ankle right away. I have a hunch there's something going on in there."

I got the X-ray machine and took some shots of Pistol's pastern, the area where I knew he had arthritic changes—ringbone. While Lonny and I waited for them to develop, I got out the two previous sets of X rays I'd taken over the last few years. They showed that the ringbone was getting steadily worse, which was more or less what you would expect.

114

The new X rays, when we looked at them, proved my hunch correct. It didn't give me much pleasure. "He's got a bone chip in there," I told Lonny, showing him where to look on the filmy gray print. "I don't know. This might be the end of his career as a rope horse."

"So, what do we do?"

"You've got a couple of choices. You can keep him on bute awhile, see if he'll stabilize and get better, or you can nerve him. There's not much point in taking the chip out, I don't think. It's not doing any harm where it is. But this horse was only bor- derline sound to begin with. This extra trauma might be the last straw."

"Will nerving him make him sound again?"

"Maybe. But we'd have to sever the nerves from the ankle down, which means his whole foot would be numb. He wouldn't be safe to ride."

"So, either way, he's probably due to be retired."

"Yeah. I'm afraid so."

Both of us stared at the big gelding. He regarded us calmly back, his wise, old eyes patient and unperturbed. Pistol had been hauled all over the western United States in his team- roping career; he'd seen it and done it all. Not much upset him.

"He won't like it," Lonny said sadly. "He doesn't want to re- tire."

"I know."

We both knew the horse loved to go. Living at his ease in a pasture would be pleasant for him, but not the same as being campaigned. Pistol was a trooper. He knew where he be- longed—going down the road to another roping.

Lonny sighed. "Well, he deserves as many good years as he has left. He's been a great horse. I'll keep him at home in the corral for a while, until he's moving around OK, and then we'll see where we're at. I'll do what's right for him."

"I know you will." I smiled up at Lonny, thinking that this was one of the nicest things about him—his heart was in the right place. Where many ropers would have chickened the horse once he was no longer useful, Lonny would keep him and care for him. It was one of the reasons we were together. Lonny loved his horses.

I gave Pistol some bute intravenously, just to make him feel better, and Lonny loaded him in the trailer. I was about to suggest lunch when the receptionist dashed out the back door of the office.

"Gail, Lisa Bennett just called and she's got an emergency. She said someone let all the horses out of their corrals. One of them got into the feed room and ate a bunch of grain, she thinks. She says he's colicked—pretty bad."

"Tell her I'm on my way."

FIFTEEN

I drove to the Bennett Ranch as fast as the law allowed; even so, it took me forty-five minutes to get there. Lone Oak was just that far away. I arrived to find a small group of people gathered in the barnyard. Glen, Al Borba, Tim, and Susan Slater stood in a confrontational square. Lisa was leading Chester in circles.

My heart sank. Not Chester. Damn. I observed him closely as Lisa led him in my direction. His expression was alert and he wasn't sweating. Good signs.

"He's better," Lisa announced. "Maybe he didn't get much grain. He couldn't have been in there very long."

"What happened" I asked her as I took the horse's pulse and respiration.

"Someone let all the horses out of their pens this morning. Al said everything was normal when he fed, and sometime between then and ten o'clock, when Dad went down to the barn, someone came along and did this."

Chester's pulse and respiration were only slightly elevated. While I watched, he started pawing the ground and acting like he wanted to roll. Lisa got him moving again. "That's what he's been doing," she said over her shoulder.

"Is he the only sick horse?" I was filling a syringe with banamine.

"Yeah. The others were just milling around. But he's too smart for his own good. He opened the latch and got in the feed room. He knows where we keep the grain. He was eating it when I found him."

Too much grain all at once was a sure recipe for colic, and maybe founder, too. "How much did he get?" I asked.

"It's hard to tell; the grain's in a big barrel. Not a whole lot, though."

"I'm going to give him a shot of painkiller, and we'll pump some mineral oil down him. Hopefully that will do it. He doesn't look too bad."

Chester accepted the injection in his jugular vein and the tube down his nose quietly, and I pumped the mineral oil into his stomach. "You'll need to keep a good eye on him for the next few hours," I told Lisa. "The banamine will wear off slowly, and if he starts to show symptoms of pain, we'll have to get right on it."

She nodded seriously as she stroked the horse's neck. Loud voices from the direction of the group around Glen made us both turn. Susan was declaiming again.

"What you're doing is cruel and inhumane," she announced to Glen. "I hear those poor cattle bawling every night."

"Oh, brother." Lisa rolled her eyes.

"What's going on?" I asked her.

"We're shipping all the steers at the beginning of next week, so we've been gathering the cattle and keeping them in these little holding pastures near the barn. Some of them are being weaned off their mothers, so they're bawling. Susan can hear it from her house. She thinks we're torturing the cattle."

I listened to Glen begin a fairly patient explanation of the logistics of cattle ranching. How the grass was done for the year and the cattle needed to be gathered and moved—otherwise they would starve.

"Do you think she let the horses out of their pens?" I asked Lisa quietly. "Freedom for animals and all that?"

Lisa looked confused. "She could have, I suppose. But would she come right back up here and start yelling at Dad?"

"Who knows?"

Susan's voice was raised again. "You're just shipping these poor little animals off to be slaughtered. It's morally wrong."

Glen's voice was still patient. "So just what do you want me to do with them?"

"Keep them and take care of them, of course."

There was a brief silence. Glen looked steadily at Susan, then at the pastureful of cattle behind them. "How about I give you one?" he said at last. He pointed at a big black baldy steer with black freckles on his pink nose. "That one right there. He's a real gentle steer. We call him Freckles. He'll let you pet him."

And Glen stepped up to the fence and stretched his hand slowly out to the steer, who did, indeed, allow his forehead to be rubbed. "What do you say?" Glen asked her. "I'll give him to you, and you give him a good home."

Susan sputtered. There was no other word for it. "Uh. Well. Where would I put him?"

"I don't know," Glen said evenly. "But if you want him to be happy, a pen in your backyard wouldn't be big enough. He'd need at least a quarter-acre. You'd have to feed him, of course."

Susan stared at the steer. There he was, a living, breathing animal whose life she could save. "I can't," she said miserably.

"I know you can't." Glen's voice was quiet. "I can't keep all these steers, either. I can't afford to, just like you can't afford this one."

"Then why do you buy them in the first place?"

"Would you rather they didn't exist? If people like me didn't raise beef cattle for other people to eat, they'd disappear forever. They'd be rarities in zoos. Is that what you want?"

Susan didn't say a word.

119

"What's wrong with the life I'm giving them? Sure, they're going to be butchered, but they ran around on the green grass all year, and I have every expectation they'll be killed humanely. Everyone has to die sometime."

Good point, Glen. Susan appeared worn down. Al and Tim were both staring at her with ill-concealed animosity. She glanced at Lisa and me, standing with Chester, and could see we weren't going to jump in.

Still looking at me, she asked, "Is the horse all right?"

"I think he'll be OK," I said guardedly. "Susan, you didn't let these horses out of their pens, did you?"

"Me?" She appeared honestly shocked. "I wouldn't do that."

"Well, some animal rights protesters have done things like that. I want to be sure you understand that you wouldn't be doing the horses a favor."

"I'm not *that* dumb," Susan snapped. She looked the group of us over with disdainful eyes. "I'm not giving up," she said clearly. "I'll be watching you." She marched off toward the road, the hem of her long skirt dragging in the dusty grass.

"How's Chester?" Glen asked me.

"We'll know in about four hours," I told him. "I just loaded him up on painkiller and mineral oil. So, how do you think this happened?"

"I don't know." Glen spoke reluctantly. "They were all out when I got down to the barn. Al says everything was normal at feeding time."

"Any of you see any strangers around the place?"

Lisa and Glen shook their heads negatively; Tim said, "Only that goddamn Susan."

Al's heavy voice broke in: "Anybody could have done it. I was out with the cattle. You can't see the barn from the big house. Any stranger could have driven in here and out again." Al's tone was defensively belligerent. Of course, this was his usual tone. But I wondered. Was Al anxious to prove the culprit wasn't necessarily someone who lived on the ranch?

"I think you should take this seriously," I said to Glen. "It wasn't an accident. Someone does seem to be," I searched for a better word and gave up, "stalking you. If I were you, I'd call the sheriff's department."

Glen's negative head shake was instantaneous. "I don't want to do that," he said firmly.

Our eyes met. Glen's were clear blue, with every one of his fifty-something years showing clearly in the lines around them. "I'd appreciate it if you wouldn't mention this to anybody."

"All right," I said slowly. "But if something else happens, I am going to feel free to report it, OK?"

He gave the slightest of nods. I could feel Al's and Tim's eyes drilling into me with separate intensity. I would have given a lot to be able to read their thoughts.

Glen turned to Lisa. "Put Chester in the front corral where we can keep an eye on him."

Lisa led the horse off; he looked bright and happy, for the moment anyway. The next few hours would show what the prognosis was.

"Don't feed him any hay for a while," I told Al and Glen. "If he seems OK by dinnertime, you can give him half an ordinary feeding. And if he's passed that oil by tomorrow morning, you can treat him normally again."

Everybody nodded assent. Lisa returned. "Can I buy you lunch?" she asked me.

"My turn," I told her. "But it will have to be a quick one."

"Meet you over there," she said and got in her pickup.

Two minutes later, we walked into the Saddlerack. As always, the cool air was refreshing in contrast to the heat of midday. Lisa took her usual table in the corner. Janey was behind the bar today. I could see Susan at the far end of the room, sitting with the bespectacled man she'd been with at the roping, talking animatedly.

It seemed sort of funny. Here we were, Lisa, Susan, Janey, and I, all in the same bar, seventeen years after we'd graduated from high school. We were quite a study in types. I suppose that in our high school years I was the smart one, Lisa the pretty one, Janey the sexy one, and Susan the hippie. As adults, we were not quite so typecast, but the clichés might still apply.

I stared at the four of us in turn. Lisa and I were reflected in the mirror behind the bar; we both looked a bit battered, I thought. My veterinary degree probably justified my high school label as "smart," and Lisa, despite the signs of stress, was still and probably always would be a very attractive woman. It was there in the bones of her face.

Glancing surreptitiously at Susan, I decided she looked much younger than Lisa and me; her fair skin was relatively unlined, as her hippie-esque attire was unchanged. Susan was quite recognizably the Susan of our high school years.

It was Janey who was the enigma. There she stood behind the bar—quiet, watchful, unreadable. She wore another tight T-shirt—this one white and sheer enough to reveal the black lace bra beneath it. As always, I had no idea what mysterious alchemy in her nature had produced the combination of overt sexiness blended with hostility. What in the world made Janey tick?

Her belligerent expression seemed more or less habitual, as did her father's, but whether it was the outward sign of deep resentment or merely a superficial facade I couldn't tell. Could Janey, or Al, possibly hate Glen enough to be Lisa's stalker? Sort of a have-nots hating the haves, Russian Revolution motivation? It seemed pretty far-fetched.

Still, I asked Lisa, "What time does this place open?"

"Eleven o'clock," she said promptly. "They don't do breakfast. And yeah, I've thought about that, too. But why would she?"

"Revolt of the downtrodden?" I shrugged my shoulders. "I don't know. There could be lots going on neither of us knows about. Maybe she had an affair with your dad and he dumped her."

It appeared this was the wrong thing to say. Lisa got up abruptly. "I'll go get our hamburgers."

When she returned, several minutes later, bearing lunch, I apologized. "I'm sorry, Lisa. I didn't mean to offend you."

"You didn't," she retorted. "I'm not offended; I'm paranoid. It could be true."

"You don't really think so?" I took a big bite of hamburger. I'm not usually a fan of this particular food, but I had to admit, the Saddlerack did a good job with them. Not to mention that hamburgers and hot dogs were the only things on the menu— besides steak.

Lisa seemed to be considering my question seriously. "Maybe," she said at last. "If I were married to Joyce, I'd sure run around."

Now we were back to Joyce again. "Could Joyce be your stalker?"

"I guess she could." Lisa shook her head. "Oh, Gail, lots of people could."

"It's a limited number, though," I said slowly. "I could give the police a pretty complete list."

"Dad would kill you."

"I know. And I don't want to upset him. But if one more weird thing happens, I'm going to the cops. This is getting spooky. Come on; finish that hamburger and let's go back and check on Chester."

Chester seemed OK when we got there. I told Lisa to keep a good eye on him and call me if he got worse, then climbed back in my truck.

Lisa stood by my door, a slightly desperate look on her face. "Gail, I'm sure you're tired of this, but we're having a practice roping tomorrow night, for the Rancher's Days roping."

"The Rancher's Days roping?"

"Dad's big roping. He has it every year, the week he ships the cattle. It's this weekend."

I remembered. But still, "You're having a big roping here this weekend? Don't you think that's asking for trouble?"

"I know." Lisa looked miserable. "But Dad refuses to cancel it. He's had it every year for over twenty years now."

"Yeah," I said slowly.

"So would you consider coming up to practice with us tomorrow night and then rope with me in the big roping? That way you could keep an eye on things." The words tumbled out of Lisa in a rush.

"I haven't done a lot of good so far," I told her.

"But I feel safer when you're around."

"I'll think about it, Lisa. If Lonny will haul our horses up here, I'll try and come practice tomorrow night. But if anything else happens, I'm warning you, I'm going to the cops."

"That's OK with me. Dad's the one who's going to skin you alive. Thanks, Gail."

"See you tomorrow," I said.

SIXTEEN

Tuesday did not begin auspiciously. I spent the morning with one of my least favorite clients, preg-checking her herd of forty broodmares. A pregnancy check on a mare is no big deal, if you have a set of stocks handy or the mare is gentle. Amber St. Claire had no stocks, however, and several of her mares were downright rank.

In order to check a mare, I had to stand directly behind her and thrust my arm (encased in a plastic sheath) up her rectum all the way to my shoulder. Thus I could palpate the cervix and uterus and determine if a mare was bred or open. Naturally, such a position causes a veterinarian to become extremely vulnerable to being kicked. Without stocks, I normally tranquilized any mare whose disposition I was unsure of. Amber, however, wouldn't hear of this.

It wasn't concern for her horses' possible reaction to the drug; Amber didn't want to pay for any "extras." "If you tranquilize them, it's on Jim, not me," she said.

I bit my tongue on, The hell it is, and said, as politely as I could manage, "It's standard procedure."

"Not at my place," she snapped back. "Go ahead and do them or I'll find a more capable vet."

I turned away, doing my best to hide what amounted to outright fury. If the decision had been up to me, I would have dispensed with Amber's business then and there, but I knew Jim was not going to see it my way. Instead, I simply motioned at Amber's stallion manager to lead the first mare up. Maybe I'd be lucky.

I wasn't. The fourth mare I examined launched a savage blow at my midsection. I jerked sideways reflexively and she caught me on the thigh instead of in the guts, but it still hurt like hell.

Limping in circles, I cursed the mare and Amber impartially but inaudibly. When I could control my voice, I said, I hoped quietly and firmly, to Amber, "The rest of these mares get tranquilized."

She didn't say a word. No doubt she was worried I'd sue her. Good. Let her worry.

Tranquilized, the rest of the herd presented no problems, but I returned to the clinic knowing full well that Amber's phone call would have gotten there before me. Sure enough, Jim motioned me into his office as soon as I walked in the door.

"I know; I know," I said wearily. "Amber just called to tell you I'm an incompetent veterinarian."

Jim's brief grin came and went. "How did you know?"

I recounted my adventures briefly and finished up with, "I'm not preg-checking any more questionable mares without tranquilizing them. I don't care what the client wants. My whole thigh's black-and-blue."

"Gail, we can't afford to antagonize clients like Amber St. Claire."

"You preg-check her mares next time. You can do them without tranquilizers, if you want."

Silence followed that remark. "Just do your best to get along with her," Jim said at last.

I shrugged. He knew as well as I did that I was right. It was just one more battle in our never-ending employer–employee struggle. Jim was as tight with money as Amber St. Claire, and his work ethic was Puritan in its intensity. The only reason he cut me any slack at all was that I had lasted with him for almost five years—a world's record. No other vet had stuck it out for longer than six months.

I endured Jim for a number of reasons—not least because I wanted to stay in Santa Cruz and Jim was the only competent horse vet in the area. I couldn't afford to open my own practice and, to be fair, Jim was more than competent; he was unsurpassed as a diagnostician. I'd learned a tremendous amount in my five years of working under him.

To top it all off, I'm stubborn. I was determined not to give up and quit, and Jim, for his part, seemed at least halfway pleased to have found someone who could keep up with his work schedule. Despite the fact that he paid low wages, expected long hours, and had a tendency to shift the difficult clients off on me, we got along. Mostly because I made sure of it.

Still, Jim irritated me at times. And this was one of them. I was further annoyed when I climbed back into my truck for the next call, turned on the air conditioner, and heard only a dead rattle. No cold air. Of course. I'd forgotten. The air conditioner was broken, and Jim had declined to fix it, saying we didn't need one in this climate.

I rolled the windows down, and a hot wind blew restlessly around me. It was better than nothing. Four hours and six calls later I was not so sanguine.

"Damn you, Jim." I thumped the dashboard in annoyance, hoping something would fall into place and the air conditioner would kick in. The temperature was in the nineties.

At least I was done for the day. I headed for Lonny's place, wishing I had time to go home and take a cool shower. But I had promised Lisa I would go to this practice roping, and Lonny had agreed to haul the horses up there. I needed to hurry.

It was six o'clock when we drove into the Bennett Ranch. I looked carefully at the colorful tangle of trucks and trailers parked in the field next to the arena. About a dozen rigs. A few I recognized; most I didn't.

Lonny parked and we got out and unloaded Burt and Gunner. As we saddled, I smelled the familiar roping arena smell. A summer evening smell. Horses and cattle and dust. People stood in little clusters by their rigs, talking, roping a dummy steer, smoking cigarettes, drinking beer. A few kids ran around. And everywhere there were horses. I smiled to myself. A roping arena felt like home.

Getting on Gunner, I rode over to the barnyard. Glen, Tim, and Lisa were saddling up. "Hey." Glen gave me his straight look, a smile that was more the intent of a smile than any perceptible motion of his facial muscles. He pulled the cinch tight on Smoke. I looked at the horse a minute, admiring him.

A registered Quarter Horse, Smoke was as good-looking as a stud gets, his dark blue-gray color a perfect complement to his little head, his massive, powerful rump, his strong shoulder and curved neck. Even with his ears pinned as they were now, annoyed at the pressure of the cinch, he looked noble, a horse straight out of an old painting.

Glen caught my gaze and I smiled. "He sure is a nice-looking horse."

Glen smiled back. "He's a good one." He slapped Smoke's neck with affectionate pride.

The stallion stood quietly for this, as he did for most things. Glen used him just as if he were a gelding, which was good, if you could get away with it. I'd heard it said that stallions were either lazy or crazy, which was as handy a description as I could come up with. The bottom line was that there were stallions you could ride and rope on and treat like a horse and there were those you had better never take your eye off if you wanted to live to a ripe old age. Smoke was in the former category.

128

I saw that Lisa was saddling Chester and said, "I take it he's OK?"

"He passed the oil this morning, and he's seemed normal all day. I'm just going to rope a couple on him."

"Sounds good." Turning Gunner, I rode back toward the arena, taking a look around to see who was there. Mostly local ranchers, it seemed, several of whom I recognized.

Pat Domini rode by on her big high-headed gelding, a horse she called Dragon, an immensely powerful beast who was one of the best head horses I knew of. His color, a solid dark red, technically called liver chestnut, combined with his size, gave him an oddly imposing presence, added to which he was a high-powered, snorty sucker with a way of looking at people as though they were insignificant ants to which he was personally indifferent. Dragon seemed a particularly fitting name.

Though Pat was a tall woman, she looked small on Dragon's back. I smiled a greeting at her, and she smiled back—absently, I thought. Immediately afterward she looked over her shoulder, toward the ranch entrance, and I saw her face get tense. I turned my head to find what she was looking at.

A small silver Mercedes was pulling into the field, one of the sporty two-seater type, with the top down. It looked like an elegant little toy next to the large trucks and trailers. Sitting in the driver's seat was Charles Domini.

I glanced back at Pat. She didn't exactly look glad to see her husband. Her eyes narrowed sharply, but then her face smoothed out. "Charles is here," she said to me, with a shrug in her voice.

I didn't say anything. Charles seldom roped but occasionally came to Glen's to lean on the fence and watch. I thought myself he was mostly interested in hearing the gossip.

He unfolded himself out of the Mercedes and strolled toward us. As always, he looked subtly overdressed, though he wore jeans, boots, and a long-sleeved shirt, like virtually every other older man there. It was the sheen of the shirt, the gleam of the polished boots, the flash of gold around his neck and on his wrist. Charles didn't look like a roper.

Pat rode in his direction. I turned Gunner and went the other way, missing whatever scene Charles and Pat were planning to play out. Threading through the parked rigs in the field, I headed for the gate to the arena, intending to warm Gunner up.

Walking past an unfamiliar rig, a truck with a large camper on the back, hitched to a battered stock trailer, I glanced idly in the window of the camper—and met the eyes of a face looking out. The impact was sudden and startling, like walking around a corner and finding someone with their pants down. I jerked my eyes away and moved on. But I recognized the face, all right. It was Sonny Santos in that camper.

I rode into the arena and kicked Gunner up into a lope, my mind spinning. Should I tell Glen or Lisa that Sonny was here? What good would it do? Surely I would only start a brawl.

I saw Lonny loping Burt and rode up beside him. "I need to talk to you," I said.

Before I could get any further, Lisa hailed me from over near the chutes. She rode in my direction, smiling. "We're roping together this weekend, right?"

"I guess so," I said. "If I can get Saturday off."

"So we'll practice together tonight? You don't mind me stealing her?" Lisa flashed a smile at Lonny.

"He's just got his head horse, anyway," I answered for him, "and I need a heeler. It'll work out just fine."

"How's the heel horse doing?" Lisa asked.

"He's lame," Lonny said sadly. "I think he's done."

"That's too bad. This one's for sale, if you're looking." She patted Chester's neck.

Lonny ran his eyes over the horse and nodded. "I'll watch him," he said.

"He's a good one," Lisa told Lonny. "Smart as a whip, and he wants to be a rope horse."

We all smiled in understanding and Lonny nodded again. "How much do you want for him?"

"He belongs to Dad. He's asking six thousand. Chester's by Smoke."

All of us looked over to where Glen sat on Smoke, talking to Al, who seemed to be complaining about something. He was a big bull of a man with a voice to match his bulk, and we could all hear his querulous tones. I couldn't catch the words, though.

Suddenly Lisa's gaze shifted from Glen and Al to the parking lot. Her eyes had a look of intensity that made me wonder if she'd spotted Sonny Santos roaming around. I followed the line of her vision and saw a blue Cadillac driving into the field, looking as incongruous as Charles's Mercedes. It parked near the arena, and after a minute Joyce got out carefully and walked up to the fence.

I stared. Joyce was turned out. Her immaculate sky blue pants were topped by a billowing snowy white blouse with silver sequins, and her cowboy boots and purse were white. Her ash blond hair was carefully arranged, and no doubt if I'd been close enough to see it, her makeup would be equally detailed. She looked like a TV version of a rancher's wife, totally unsuited to the dusty arena where she stood.

As we watched, Glen's jaw got a little squarer and he rode Smoke up to the fence. Lisa said, almost to herself, "What's *she* doing here?" Obviously Joyce was not a regular at practice ropings.

Glen sat on Smoke a while, talking to Joyce, then dismounted and walked off toward the barn, leading the horse. Joyce went with him. I watched Lisa follow them with her eyes until they disappeared behind the barn.

The cattle were standing in the chute, ready to go, and the ropers were looking impatient, but Al was nowhere to be seen. Lonny and Lisa and I all turned our horses in a unanimous motion and began loping them around. Time to get warmed up.

Galloping Gunner, feeling the warm evening wind in my

face, I forgot the tensions of the moment and began to relax. Maybe we would just have a good time here. It was only a roping, after all.

Five minutes later there was a light sweat on Gunner's neck and all his muscles were loose. We were ready. On the thought, I saw Glen riding toward the box on Smoke; Al stood by the chutes. "Clear the arena!" he hollered.

We all rode out the gate. Out of the corner of my eye I saw Joyce's Cadillac inching out of the field. I looked around for a glimpse of Sonny Santos, but he was nowhere in sight. My roaming gaze caught Charles Domini, leaning on the fence. He gave me his slow, unpleasant smile, the smile of a conspirator.

I looked back at Glen, riding Smoke toward the box. Even from a distance it was apparent something had upset the horse. He was tossing his head, skittering, and spooking, and his neck was wet with sweat. Glen's face was set hard and looked angry; if I hadn't known better I would have guessed that Glen had been beating on the horse. But Glen wouldn't have done that. He knew how stallions were—whipping them only caused trouble.

Still, something had happened. Smoke, usually calm and reliable, looked frantic. Glen rode him into the header's box and got him turned around by main force. Smoke wouldn't stand still; he reared up again and again. Gradually the arena got quiet as everybody focused on the man and the horse struggling in the header's box.

Smoke seemed to be getting wilder and wilder; the look in his eyes was close to panic. I didn't understand it. Smoke was a broke head horse. This much agitation was bizarre.

I could hear Lisa's voice, thin and scared. "Dad, just walk him out of there. He's freaking out."

Glen's jaw was hard. He snapped a look at the whole arena. "This son of a bitch is going to stand in this box if I have to go 'round with him all night," he said flatly.

He backed the horse up and took a firm hold of the reins.

Smoke froze for a split second, unnaturally still. Suddenly he rose up again in a rear. Only this time it was different; this time the horse went up and back all in one motion, with no hesitation, the whole weight and momentum of his body thrown backward in a last-ditch effort to escape the situation.

It happened so quickly there was hardly time for thought. First the horse hanging in the air, then dropping over backward, a flash of Glen's body moving as he threw himself sideways, then the ominous crash of Smoke falling into the fence behind the header's box.

The horse was down. I couldn't see Glen. Then the horse was scrambling to his feet and galloping off at a dead run; he looked OK. Glen slowly raised himself to a sitting position as several people converged on him. I could hear his words: "I'm all right."

Climbing off Gunner, I handed the reins to Lonny and went after Smoke. The stallion was charging up and down the back fence of the arena frantically, looking as if he might try to jump out. I walked in his direction, talking quietly in an attempt to soothe him while I assessed his expression. He looked scared to death.

Eventually he ran into a corner and stopped for a minute. His eyes were wide, his nostrils huge and puffing, and his forelegs were trembling. His coat was so wet it was dripping. He stared at me apprehensively, as though I'd come to eat him, rather than catch him. I thought his behavior totally uncharacteristic.

I advanced toward him quietly, murmuring meaningless words. He was shaking where he stood. Gently I reached up and pulled the reins over his head and started to lead him off. He scrambled backward against the pressure, looking like he might flip over backward again.

I dropped the reins and let him go. He ran a few steps and stopped, still trembling. I just stood there and watched him. A voice from the sidelines broke into my attention: "What's wrong with him?"

133

It was Susan. She stood by the fence, staring at me and Smoke, her eyes sharp and suspicious.

"He's just scared," I said quietly.

Susan looked unconvinced.

Shifting my attention back to Smoke, I spoke in my most reassuring tone. "You'll be OK," I told him. "Just relax. That's a good boy."

Smoke was still trembling. White foam dripped from his mouth. Another voice cut into my concentration: "So, why don't you catch him?"

Janey's voice. She stood by Susan, and both their eyes were fixed on me and the horse.

"He needs to think it over," I said. "He's still pretty upset."

I watched Smoke for another couple of minutes. He finally seemed to let down a little. Once again, I reached for the reins and asked him for a step forward. He tensed up a little, but he took one. Then another. Then he was following me, shaky and still nervous, but controllable.

Glen was standing in the header's box, surrounded by Lisa, Tim, and Al. I could hear Lisa's voice, sharply raised: "Dad, enough is enough."

More talk and then Al bellowed out, "Everybody go home! We're not gonna practice after all. Glen's going down to the hospital." Al looked grimly satisfied, I thought, like an Old Testament prophet of doom after disaster had struck.

I did a quick reconnaissance. Charles Domini's silver Mercedes was gone. The rig with the camper on it was just bumping out of the parking lot. I couldn't see who was driving it. Couldn't see any faces peering out of the camper windows, either.

People started loading their horses, getting ready to go home. Lonny still sat on Burt, holding Gunner. Pat Domini was next to him, on Dragon. Both of them watched Glen hobble slowly across the arena, leaning on Tim's shoulder.

Tim helped his father into the passenger side of his green

Sixball truck, and they drove out. On the way to the hospital, I presumed. I led Smoke over to Lisa.

The horse was still nervous, but he no longer seemed irrational. "We need to talk," I told Lisa. "Right away."

Lisa looked pretty distraught. "I've got to get these horses unsaddled and fed," she said.

"I'll help," I told her. "Will you drive me home?"

"Sure."

I let Lonny know what my plans were; he agreed to take Burt and Gunner home and wait to hear from me. Then I helped Lisa unsaddle Smoke, Rosie, Roany, and Chester. I watched Smoke for another few minutes after I turned him out in his pen; he seemed a little restless but basically all right. He was willing to put his head down and eat his hay, anyway.

Eventually we were done. I got in the pickup with Lisa, and she drove it up the hill, past the big house, dark and quiet. I could see no sign of Joyce's Cadillac. Lisa made no motion to stop.

We made the trip to Lisa's house in silence. We didn't arrive there in silence, though. I could hear the sharp barks of the two Queenslands over the noise of the engine as Lisa pulled into the yard. Brisk, happy barks, barks of greeting.

Lisa called to them to hush as we got out of the truck and I followed her into the yard. Joey sniffed my leg; Rita aimed a soft, fake nip at my heels.

Lisa walked into the house, disappeared into the kitchen, and reappeared with tumblers of ice and amber liquid. "Brandy and soda," she said briefly.

I nodded, accepted a glass, and sat down on the couch, breathing in the warm, familiar smell of dog. Some people would have said the room stank. To me, it smelled pleasant and comforting.

Lisa sat down in one of her fat chairs, her movements jerky and abrupt. She stared into space for several seconds, holding her drink but not drinking it. I took a long swallow of mine.

Joey sat down next to Lisa's knee, and she stroked him with

an absent hand, not looking at me or the dog or anything else that I could see. Rita walked up to me humbly, head down, ears folded back, as though apologizing for her suspicious nature. I held my hand out. She rubbed her head against it, petting herself. After a minute I stroked her forehead and scratched her behind the soft, pointed ears.

Lisa finally looked at me. "It wasn't an accident, was it?"

"No," I said. "Somebody gave that horse something."

"You're sure?"

"Pretty sure. There was a small mark on his neck that could have been an injection site, and I don't think there's any other reasonable explanation for his behavior."

"What could cause that?"

"Any one of a number of things. Epinephrine, amphetamines, prostaglandins. They could all cause agitation and excitement."

"How could somebody manage to give it to him?"

"Glen led Smoke away right before the roping. He went off to talk to Joyce, it looked like. Smoke was out of sight of the arena, behind the barn, for several minutes. When Glen came back, he looked mad and the horse looked crazy. Something happened."

"Could somebody really give him a shot that quickly?"

"Sure they could. I could. You sort of palm the shot in your hand so the horse, or other people, can't see it. You reach up to the horse's neck like you're going to pet him and just slip the injection in the jugular vein. It doesn't take three seconds. I do it all the time on difficult horses." It was the method I used on Thunder, for instance.

"And the shot would take effect that fast?"

"You bet. A shot in the jugular vein takes effect in a matter of minutes."

"So, what do we do now?" Lisa sounded confused.

"Tell the cops," I said promptly. "I've got a bad feeling about all this."

"OK. But we have to tell Dad first," Lisa said. "He'd never forgive me if we went to the cops without telling him."

"All right. Where is he? Down at the hospital?"

"Yeah. I made him go down there to be checked out. His ankle was swelling up. It got caught between Smoke and the fence."

"I guess I can call him in the morning," I said doubtfully. "I wouldn't talk to the sheriff's department before then. In which case, I ought to get going, Lisa. I've got to be at work tomorrow."

It was black dark as we left Lisa's house; stars were white pinpricks in the steady sky. No man-made glow diminished the emptiness, and I had the vivid sense that I could see those other galaxies spinning through space.

We drove out of Lisa's little valley without incident, but Lisa braked as we approached Glen's house. Lights were on. Tim's truck was parked in the drive. "They're back," she said. "Should we go in?"

"Might as well."

I felt hesitant, though, as I followed Lisa through Glen's back door. I was an outsider, an intruder in this strange family conference. I didn't belong.

Glen's huge living room was dim, lit only by the cold light of the TV. The flickering blue-white glow showed Glen and Tim sitting in two armchairs in front of the set. They appeared to be watching some sort of sitcom; I could hear the sound of canned laughter.

Lisa said, "Hi, Dad," and turned on a lamp. I could see the men had beers in their hands. Glen had some sort of wrap around his ankle, and there were crutches leaning against the back of his chair.

"How's your leg?" Lisa asked anxiously.

"Sprained. They think it could take a while to heal. I may be on crutches for a month." Glen's voice was emotionless.

"We need to talk to you," Lisa said, her face tight with concern.

137

Glen looked quietly up at her. "All right."

"Gail thinks Smoke was drugged. We need to go to the police. Now."

"You've got to be kidding." Tim's slow drawl. "That stud horse just got excited. Studs do that. They're like pit bulls. You push the wrong button, they go nuts."

"Bullshit," Lisa snapped at him. "That was no accident and you know it."

"I don't know," Glen intervened. "A stallion will do that, occasionally."

Lisa looked straight at Tim, ignoring her father. "Damn it, what's wrong with you? Dad almost got killed in another accident, and you want to act like nothing's going on."

"Give it a rest, Lisa." Tim's voice was flat and hard; the careless quality had disappeared.

"I will *not* give it a rest. This is serious." Lisa virtually stamped her foot.

There was a tense quiet. Tim stretched his legs out slowly, a purposefully relaxed gesture. "You're crazy, Lisa. You're just plain crazy. You and Gail both. Who's going to drug Dad's horse for God's sake? All this stuff is just stupid. Dad got in a wreck and it's no big deal." Tim got to his feet abruptly. "I've had enough of this bullshit." We all heard the door slam as he left the room.

I turned back to Glen. "I'm sorry to be causing trouble," I said, "but I do think someone drugged your horse. And I think it's time we went to the sheriff's department with this."

Glen shook his head heavily. "No cops."

"Glen, your life may be in danger here. Something very strange is going on."

"Can you prove someone drugged Smoke?"

I hesitated. "Maybe. I could run a few blood tests. But epinephrine would be undetectable. Amphetamines we might catch."

"So you can't necessarily prove anyone did anything."

"That's true."

"Then the cops won't help you, anyway. And I don't want them involved."

I started to open my mouth, but he held up his hand, pushing my words away. "Gail, it's my life and I don't want any cops mixed up in it. I know you mean well, but leave it alone."

I stared at him for a long minute. He wouldn't meet my eyes. Was he some kind of masochistic martyr, I wondered, determined to suffer on until he was killed? Or more likely, was he just plain afraid to find out who the stalker was? Surely it couldn't be distaste for scandal that was causing him to put up with this harassment.

I glanced over at Lisa. All the fire seemed to have gone out of her; she looked mute and miserable. No help there.

"All right," I told Glen. "I'll respect your wishes. But I want you to know, I think this is serious. Someone very sick is behind this, and there are a limited number of people who it could be. Think about it." Turning to Lisa, I said, "Would you mind taking me home?"

"Sure." Lisa seemed barely able to get the word out. I started to follow her out of the room, and a thought occurred to me. "Is Joyce here?" I asked Glen.

"No, she went out." His tone indicated there would be no more information forthcoming. It was time to leave.

I left. Lisa made some show of apologizing while she drove me home, but I shushed her. "It's OK," I said. "I understand. He's pretty stressed. But, Lisa, keep your eyes open. I'm really worried."

"I know," she said. "So am I. But you see how he is. I just don't know what to do. You'll come up this weekend?"

"I'll try," I promised.

SEVENTEEN

Wednesday morning dawned bright and shiny. I sighed as I looked out my kitchen window at the tangle of redwood branches, gleaming green in the sun's first sharp rays. Not a trace of fog. Just how long was this heat spell going to last?

I made a pot of coffee and poured some into my favorite blue willow cup, then added honey and cream. This honey-and-cream thing was a new development for me, one I'd learned from Lonny. I was enjoying it.

Lonny. Damn. What in hell was I going to do about Lonny? The ball's in his court, I reminded myself. What was Lonny going to do about Sara? While he was deciding, I remained in limbo. Lonely limbo.

Settling myself at one end of the couch, I took a sip of coffee and stared out the window at the sunny morning, not seeing a thing. My life, once so simple and straightforward, had suddenly gotten impossibly convoluted. Did I want to marry Lonny? If I didn't agree to marry him, would I lose him completely? Could I handle going back to a solitary life?

So many questions to which I had no ready answers. I stared around my familiar living room, wondering what the future was going to be like. If this house sold quickly, I would have to figure out what I wanted pretty damn fast. I'd always assumed I could move in with Lonny, at least temporarily. But now, now what?

I wasn't sure. But I could hear a steady refrain, somewhere in my inner ear, that voted for independence. Buy your own place, it said. Let Lonny sort things out for himself.

Well, I could do that. And if he sorted himself away from me, I'd have to live with it.

Oh, hell. I took a long swallow of coffee, feeling intolerably confused, an unusual emotion for me. I wanted to feel secure in my direction and goals, as I had been for many years. I definitely did not want to feel like this.

Jerking my mind firmly off the subject of my own future, I went back to my other most pressing problem—Glen and his stalker. What I ought to do, I told myself, is call the cops. Call Jeri Ward, a woman I knew who was a detective with the Santa Cruz County sheriff's department. Tell her my story. Ask her what I should do.

I replayed this scenario in my mind. How in the world was I going to make dead colts, tractors left in gear, open gates, and irrational rope horses sound like anything other than the normal twists and turns of life on a ranch? Jeri was not going to be impressed with the fact that Glen had actually managed to sprain his ankle.

Not to mention Glen would be furious if he got a call from the sheriff's department. At me and Lisa both. And what good was it going to do? They would hardly mount a twenty-four-hour guard on him.

And yet I was sure that the accidents were not accidents. The stalker was real. And I didn't think he or she was done yet. If only I had a strong conviction who it was, I could try confrontation. At the very least, I could tell Lisa and Glen what I thought.

The trouble was, I had no such conviction. What I had was

half a dozen suspects. I rolled them around in my mind. First one would pop to the top, then another. No consensus.

The obvious choice was Sonny Santos. Lisa, I knew, believed Sonny was the culprit. But Lisa was paranoid about Sonny. Still, Sonny had been hiding in that camper. What else could it mean?

That he was hanging around hoping for a glimpse of Lisa. I supplied a further answer: hoping perhaps for a chance to talk to her, maybe even abduct her. It was quite possible that Sonny was entirely ignorant of the attacks on Glen and was interested only in some plan of his own concerning Lisa.

Charles Domini. I didn't like Charles. But was it really his style to sneak around someone else's ranch digging holes in their arena?

Susan Slater? I had a hard time believing it. Susan seemed to me to be basically well-intentioned, just misinformed. I honestly couldn't see Susan doing something that might result in a dead horse.

I could, however, imagine Al Borba killing a horse. I doubted he would turn a hair. But what motive did he really have?

And Janey. I was damned if I could figure Janey out. I gave a moment's serious consideration to the notion that she might really have had an affair with Glen—the woman scorned and all that.

Of course, there was Joyce. She was Lonny's choice. But Joyce had been married to Glen for close to thirty years. Why start stalking him now?

But Tim, Tim made sense. I didn't like this thought. Tim had been right at hand when every single accident had taken place. And Tim had a motive as old as Oedipus. Not to mention the sense I'd had lately that the violence in Tim was barely suppressed. Tim was very clearly angry at Lisa and her insistence on a stalker. It did, indeed, make sense.

Shit. Maybe Glen was right to persist with his head firmly in the sand. How could he face the knowledge that his own son might be trying to kill him? The thought made me shiver, and I put my cup down so abruptly that a little coffee spilled on the marble top of the antique dresser. I wiped it off absently with the cuff of my sweatshirt. Tim couldn't be trying to kill Glen.

Was the stalker actually trying to kill Glen, after all? It didn't seem clear. The dead foal, for instance, was no threat to Glen's physical well-being. But drugging Smoke, now, that could easily have resulted in a fatal accident. What in the hell was the stalker after?

Making Glen's life miserable, apparently, and he/she had no objections to said life being short, as well. I got up suddenly from the couch and went to the phone, determined to call Jeri Ward, after all. But I hung up after punching the first two numbers. What could I say? What good would it do?

I was now running late. Grabbing a clean shirt and a pair of jeans, I dressed in a hurry, my mind still churning away on the subject of the stalker. I thought about it all the way to work— that is, until I pulled into the driveway of the clinic. Pandemonium was the only word for the back lot.

A horse, or rather a large pony, was thrashing about at the end of his lead rope and flung himself down on the ground as I watched. The woman standing by the horse trailer was half-shouting, half-screaming, the man with her was ineffectually trying to calm her, and Jim was in the process of cutting the pony's lead rope so the animal didn't throttle himself. "Epinephrine!" Jim yelled at me at the top of his voice.

I ran to the back of my truck, sorting things out in my head as I went. Epinephrine. That meant the pony had had a massive allergic reaction to something, maybe a vaccination. I filled a syringe with ten cc's of epinephrine and ran toward Jim. Anaphylactic shock was nothing to dawdle about. The pony would be dead if we didn't hurry.

The animal was flat on his side now, legs twitching and shuddering. Jim had cut the lead rope and was sitting on the pony's head, holding the neck as still as possible so I could get the shot in the jugular vein. I put one knee on the pony's neck, rolled my fingers across the groove to find the vein, put the needle in, and saw reassuring drops of blood well up. I injected the shot.

Jim let out a deep breath, but we all stayed frozen in place, waiting for the medication to take effect. I could hear the woman's sobs in the background.

A minute passed. The pony quit moving his legs. I glanced at his flanks. In and out, in and out, steady, regular breaths. Jim looked at me. Slowly we both got up. The pony's eyes were wide and startled. In another second, he scrambled to his feet.

"Damn." Jim shook his head as he tied the lead rope back together. "First one I've ever had to do that."

"What was it?" I asked.

"Penicillin," he said. "He's got a puncture wound." He pointed to the animal's knee, and I could see, now that all the scuffling was over, that the knee was grossly swollen. There was a small surface wound. "It goes in about two inches," Jim said. "I gave him a shot of penicillin and he reacted to it."

I nodded. Jim turned to the clients and began explaining what had happened; I backed away as unobtrusively as I could. Reactions to penicillin were rare but not unknown. Jim would prescribe another antibiotic, and all would probably be well. But it would no doubt take him a while to reassure the woman.

I didn't blame her. Seeing your animal almost die before your eyes is scary, and many of our clients, normally quite sane people, became almost irrational in the face of their horse's distress. Coping with the people and their degree of upset was a big part of this job, sometimes the most wearing part. Leaving Jim to his work, I headed into the office to check the schedule.

The receptionist met me at the door. "Gail, there's a colic up in Felton. Lacy Carson. She says it's bad."

"Tell her I'll be right there."

Back in the truck and up Graham Hill Road. I pulled in Lacy Carson's driveway and breathed the sweet, earthy smell of red-

145

wood dust already warm in the air. Lacy was standing by the corral fence and walked to meet me. "I'm afraid you'll have to put him down," she said.

A woman in her sixties, Lacy was a competent horsewoman of the old school; she seldom called a vet unless the situation was dire, preferring to treat her horses herself. Her knowledge was sufficient for most situations, but I had several times found myself at odds with her when my treatment of choice was one she'd never heard of. Fortunately, Lacy was as intelligent as she was hardheaded, and most of the time I was able to convince her that newer ideas weren't necessarily bad.

"So what's going on here?" I asked her.

She waved a hand at the corral. "Colicked," she said. "He got sick yesterday and I gave him some banamine and he seemed to come out of it. He was fine last night. But this morning he's worse. You might as well put him down. I'm not going to do surgery."

None of this was unreasonable. Banamine was frequently the best treatment for colic, and the fact that Lacy wouldn't contemplate surgery to fix the horse made sense, too. Colic surgery these days costs roughly five thousand dollars, often more than a given horse is worth. Not to mention the recovery period is almost a year and many horses never do recover.

Dealing with colic and its ramifications was my most frequent occupation; colic, which is a generic term for any sort of digestive disturbance in a horse, is the most common cause of death in the equine species. Nature has provided horses with a digestive tract that becomes upset easily, and since horses can't vomit, the incidences of upset stomach turning into ruptured guts are all too common.

I stared at the paint gelding in the corral. He was staggering around, his head stuck straight up in the air, walking blindly. He was clearly in distress, but his behavior seemed odd.

Lacy picked up a halter from the rail. "Get the kill shot," she said. "I'm tired of watching him suffer."

"All right." I went to the truck.

Lacy got the horse out of the corral, and I walked up to him and put a hand on him, feeling the stiff, trembling muscles under the wet hide. This horse was suffering, no doubt about that. "I'm going to give him a shot of muscle relaxant first," I said. "I don't like to give a kill shot to a horse in this degree of distress; they react too violently."

Lacy nodded her head without a word. She was smoking a cigarette and her face was expressionless; she appeared completely unmoved by the horse's plight. I knew better. Lacy Carson had owned horses all her life, and she was fond of them. She just wasn't big on showing emotion.

I injected the six cc's of ace promazine in the horse's jugular vein; in a minute I could see the effect. The horse relaxed and looked quietly around him. In another minute he put his head down and began eating the grass that grew on the verge of the driveway, appearing for all the world like a perfectly normal horse.

Lacy looked away. I stared at the gelding. A red-and-white paint, he was short-coupled and stocky, with lots of white on his face and blue eyes. I noticed that the rims around the eyes had a faintly yellowish cast.

Stepping up to the horse, I took hold of his muzzle and lifted his upper lip. His gums, too, were yellowish.

I looked back at Lacy. "I'm not going to put this horse down," I said. "There's something else going on here. This isn't a normal colic. Has anything unusual happened to this horse in the last few days?"

Lacy shook her head, her eyes on the gelding. "I had him out yesterday; I was going to take him to a team penning. He started acting funny while I was getting ready to go, pawing the ground and sticking his head up in the air. I finally decided he was colicked and gave him some banamine. The rest you know."

"What have you been feeding him?"

147

"Alfalfa hay."

This wasn't unusual. Most horses in Central California are fed a diet of mainly alfalfa. "So, nothing's new in his feed?"

"No." Lacy sounded doubtful. "I did give him a vaccination the day before yesterday."

Bingo. "What sort of vaccination?" I asked.

"The usual. Four-way. I knew he was going to this penning and I wanted him current on his shots."

It all made perfect sense. *Four-way* was a horseman's short-hand for a vaccination that contained inoculations for tetanus, eastern and western sleeping sickness, and flu. Occasionally horses reacted to this shot. Usually reactions were mild— swelling at the injection site, a low-grade fever. But once in a great while these unfavorable reactions could affect the liver.

"See the yellow cast to his mucous membranes," I told Lacy. "I think he's having liver problems."

"What do I do?"

"Get him off alfalfa hay, for one thing. Feed him straight oat hay, nothing else." I studied the horse's muzzle. As I had more than half suspected, the pinkish unpigmented skin asso-ciated with his white hair looked raw and sunburned, another manifestation of liver failure. "Do you have a stall you can put him in, out of the sun?"

"Yes."

I pointed out the sunburning on the gelding's face and told Lacy to keep him in the stall. Prescribing rest and low-energy feed for the next couple of days, I gave her some antibiotics, took a sample of blood from the horse, and asked her to call me if he took a turn for the worse.

Lacy nodded agreement.

"He might not get better," I said. "We may still have to put him down. But let me run this blood and see what I come up with. I'll call you."

Getting in my truck, I started off down her driveway, pick-ing up the car phone and punching the office number as I went.

It must have been my day for allergic reactions. The receptionist sent me out to see a horse with a massive outbreak of hives.

This mare was swollen all over when I got there—huge welts all over her body, her face puffy, her expression miserable. She belonged to a teenage girl named Sharon who adored her. Chance, so named because she'd been bought on a whim at the livestock auction and it was only a lucky chance that had saved her from the killers, was a sweet little Appaloosa who was the champion gymkhana horse in these parts.

Sharon was crying steadily, trying to conceal her tears by looking away. "Will she die?" she asked.

"No," I said firmly. "This is probably a reaction to a bug bite, maybe a bee sting. I see this kind of thing all the time." I gave Sharon a dozen packets of azium, an orally administered steroid. "Just sprinkle this on her feed morning and night for the next few days. She should go back to normal right away. I'll give her a shot to get her started."

I injected twenty cc's of dexamethasone in the mare's jugular vein, reassured Sharon some more, and got back in the truck.

Next was a horse who'd been kicked on the stifle and had a gaping wound that needed to be stitched. Then a jumper who had gone suddenly lame in both front feet; it turned out this horse had been shod the day before by an inexperienced farrier who'd pared away a little too much sole. Then out to see an old horse who was having trouble eating and was getting thin. A routine check of this gelding's teeth showed he was missing a molar; the opposing tooth, meeting no resistance, had grown until it was cutting into the animal's gums when he tried to chew. It took me half an hour working with bolt cutters and rasp, but I eventually managed to chop the offending tooth off and smooth it up.

On and on it went. I had no time to rest, no time to think. One thing can certainly be said for being a horse vet—it keeps you busy.

The rest of the day and the days that followed passed seam-

149

lessly, veterinary problems filling my thoughts. I didn't hear from Lisa. Lonny and I had dinner together twice; nothing was said about our future. I asked for and got Saturday off. Jim wasn't pleased, but he acquiesced. I'd covered for him several times last month while he took his family on various expeditions. He owed me and he knew it.

I kept worrying about Glen's stalker. I was convinced someone was behind the long chain of purported accidents, and I was certain there would eventually be another. Several times I started again to call the police, but I always weakened. I didn't have one shred of evidence to prove my case. So I waited. Mistakenly, it turned out.

EIGHTEEN

Eight o'clock on Saturday morning Lonny and I pulled in the familiar Bennett Ranch entrance. The heat wave had finally broken; a fog bank sat leaden and gray over the Pacific coast, cooling the air. Halfway up Lone Oak Road, we'd risen out of the wet mist into the sunshine, but the temperature stayed chilly; Santa Cruz County's air-conditioning system was back in working order.

The Bennett Ranch looked dew-washed and sparkling in the bright morning air, and thoughts of a stalker seemed ridiculous. Al was loading cattle in the chutes and wrapping their horns with protective leather in preparation for the roping. Lisa and Tim helped him. Lisa had brought the two Queenslands, and they ran around happily, barking and nipping at cattle whenever an opportunity presented itself.

Tim looked up from wrapping horns and smiled indifferently at the dogs. "Worthless, no-good, stubborn sons of bitches," he drawled. "I had one of them once. A Queensland heeler. You know, that was the only dog I ever really enjoyed shooting."

I looked away. I had no idea if the story was true or not. What was clear was that Tim was back in typical form. Lisa had

151

heard his comment; she merely rolled her eyes at me and kept working. Everything seemed reassuringly normal.

Trucks and trailers rumbled into the driveway in a steady trickle. Lonny and I saddled Burt and Gunner and started to warm them up. Glen appeared, still on crutches, supervising the production of the roping. In a way, I thought, it was a good thing he'd hurt his ankle; it made him easier to keep an eye on.

I loped Gunner around, swung my rope, waited for things to get going. The early-morning air was sharp and clean, and the sun gleamed in red glints on Gunner's neck. Despite the unusual circumstances, I felt a rush of excitement at the thought of the upcoming roping. Lisa was a good partner. She and I were capable of winning this thing.

I could hear the cattle banging around in the chute, then Al's voice bellowing out, "Clear the arena!" We all rode out of the pen, and Al started calling out the teams. Lisa and I were the fifth team out. I stepped off Gunner and tightened his cinch.

Gunner watched me with his bright, curious expression, and I thought, not for the first time, what a nice horse he was and how lucky I was to own him. I'd only started competing on him six months ago; before that I'd always roped on Burt, Lonny's head horse. Solid and dependable, Burt had effectively taught me to rope; when I'd developed enough confidence I'd moved on to Gunner.

Gunner was still green; I couldn't just forget about him and let him do his job, as I could with Burt. I needed to ride Gunner and support him—reinforce his training. But he was willing and cooperative, as well as fast and strong, and I loved roping on him.

Getting back on him, I swung my rope to loosen my arm and focused my mind on roping. I pictured my loop closing around the steer's horns, pictured myself dallying smoothly around the saddle horn.

I studied the people in the arena, trying to decide just how tough this roping was going to be. It was limited to residents of

Santa Cruz or Santa Clara counties, and Glen used the West Coast handicapping system. This meant ropers who had won a lot of money had to rope with people who hadn't, so the teams, theoretically, were all of the same ability. In practice, it didn't quite work out like that—there were still a few tough teams. Tim was roping with a kid from a neighboring ranch who had virtually no money won but was still a terrific heeler. And Lonny's partner was an old man named Wes Goodwin who almost never competed, thus had no winnings to speak of, but was absolutely deadly. Lisa and I would have to rope all ten steers to win this roping.

Al called out our names, and I rode Gunner into the header's box and turned him around. I could feel his heart thumping steadily, but he was calm. Lisa rode Chester into the heeler's box. "You ready?" I asked her.

"Any time," she said.

I tightened the reins on Gunner and nodded for the steer. There was the clang of the gate opening, the flash of the steer jumping forward, and then Gunner and I were after him, running full-speed down the arena.

Gunner closed the gap easily; I stood in my stirrups and swung my rope and threw. The loop went on the horns perfectly; I pulled the rope to take out the slack, dallied around the saddle horn, and reined Gunner off to the left.

I could feel the horse gather himself underneath me as he picked up the steer's weight and began to pull him; I could see that the steer was leading off easily and Lisa was in the right position. Lisa threw, and her loop went neatly in front of the steer's back legs; in another second she pulled her rope tight and I whirled Gunner around to face her. The timer dropped the flag. Nine seconds. Not bad. We could have been quicker, but it was a satisfactory start.

I rode Gunner back up toward the chutes, feeling good. Lisa rode next to me, shaking her head. "I didn't get the loop all the way under him. I was just lucky I caught two feet," she said.

153

"You did great," I told her happily.

We rode by Tim, leaning on the fence talking to Janey Borba. Her skintight T-shirt was black this morning, tucked into black Wrangler jeans, the impossibly small waist cinched with an enormous silver buckle. She looked like trash, but very attractive trash.

Lisa's head turned sharply and I followed her gaze. We both watched Glen limp around the end of the arena on his crutches. He stopped to greet Pat Domini, giving her the Glen Bennett smile. I wondered if Lisa saw, as I did, how old Glen looked and how tired. He was smiling at Pat in the same old Glen Bennett way, but something was missing. He looked like he was having to work at it.

We spent the rest of the morning roping. There were just over a hundred teams, and we all had to rope three steers before lunch. Lisa heeled all three of ours by two feet, to keep us solidly in the average, but we weren't fast. Thirty-eight seconds on three steers is not world-class. On the other hand, I was grateful I had managed to catch and turn every steer.

By noon, Tim and the sixteen-year-old neighbor kid, whose name was Billy Walsh, were leading the roping, with Lonny and Wes Goodwin a close second. There were still three steers left to rope that afternoon.

Al hollered that we were breaking for lunch, and we all lined up to eat the hamburgers that Janey and a couple of other women were selling at an impromptu snack shack. There were picnic tables set up in the shade of the lone oak, and people gathered in groups, chattering happily. A cool breeze moved about, thinning the midday heat.

I was sitting at a table with Lonny and Glen and Lisa and Tim when Joyce's Cadillac pulled into the parking lot. She got out of the car, wearing another dressy Western-type outfit, this one in shades of pink, and walked in our direction. As she approached, I could see her eyes flicking casually through the crowd; she replied to greetings here and there but initiated no conversation. She moved steadily toward our table.

I found myself studying her as she mouthed some polite, how's-everything-going comments to a man who had said hello, watching the way her eyes stayed flat. I had no idea what was going through her mind.

Her expression, as she greeted the group of us, gave nothing away. She asked if everyone was roping well, and her voice held all the warmth and interest of the time recording. I shook my head mentally. The body was lush and well preserved, the wrappings expensive, but I tended to agree with Lisa. If I were Glen, I'd have an affair. Or, better yet, a divorce.

Glen was talking to Joyce about the barbecue they were hosting tomorrow afternoon. Apparently Joyce was going shopping for food. The discussion was brief, terse, and to the point. No frills, no warmth. Joyce said good-bye to the group at large. Before she left, her eyes met mine briefly, then flickered away. " 'Bye, Joyce," I said.

"Good-bye, Gail," she answered. She was turning as she spoke, and I saw for a second, in her profile, what a pretty woman she still was. Then she was gone.

The roping went on. Horses and cattle and dust and camaraderie.

Lonny sat next to me on Burt. We watched the roping and commented on the horses and people. Burt pinned his ears grouchily at Gunner. Lonny talked to me and smiled at me and laughed with me. It felt like the old days, when we were courting.

I kept half an eye on Glen as he hobbled around; I could tell Lisa was doing the same—but somehow the stalker didn't seem real. The roping seemed real.

Lonny was roping well and consistently, and Wes Goodwin couldn't seem to miss. They went to the lead, and Lonny had a grin a mile wide. Ben and Bob Green, two brothers from

Watsonville, roped a couple of seven-second steers, which put them in second. Tim and Billy were third.

Lisa caught one foot instead of two on the sixth steer, which added five seconds onto our time. We ended up in seventh place overall for the day. There were still four more steers to rope tomorrow, and we were definitely in contention.

Lonny and I each had another hamburger, unsaddled the horses and put them in the pens Glen had offered us, then headed for the Saddlerack, along with most of the crowd. The Saddlerack had hired a band; it was going to be a party.

Dusk was just turning to dark as we pulled into the parking lot. The old building was already filled with people. Ropers in cowboy hats and ball caps, still wearing their spurs, talked and laughed around the bar; a few couples moved on the dance floor. The light was dim, and the trophy heads gazed out from the shadows through the smoky air. The people chattered and smiled and lifted their drinks. The band played.

Glen and Lonny and Lisa and I stood by the bar. Talk swirled around us. People came and went, but the subject stayed the same.

"Did you see that good-looking bald-faced bay Wes was roping on? That sure is a good son of a bitch."

"Pat and Jim would be sitting first right now if Jim would have caught that last steer."

"Earl's wife turned a good one for him; too bad Earl missed it." A laugh. "Yep, old Earl's going to be washing dishes tonight."

The talk went on as the bar got more and more crowded. The dance floor was full of couples. I ordered another beer and saw Charles and Pat Domini come in the door. Charles looked angry; Pat looked bored. I felt more than saw Glen's body straighten. But Charles and Pat walked to the other end of the bar.

The band started "Rockytop" and Tim pulled Lisa out on the dance floor. I watched them dance while Glen told Lonny about

156

a black gelding somebody had for sale as a heel horse. "He's all right," Glen said, "but he's at least twelve, and probably fourteen. How many years can you expect to get out of him?"

Lisa and Tim had danced together a lot. They moved smoothly in the in-and-out step of Western swing, twisting and turning without effort in the slick, complicated moves. Tim clowned, putting in extra flourishes, his eyes alight with fun. Tim had no inhibitions.

Most of the room was watching them dance. When the song ended, they got a round of applause. Lisa walked back toward us, looking half-embarrassed. Tim sauntered, happy and amused, turning to holler, "Stand on it!" to the guitar player, who had started another song. I laughed.

We all had a beer. I watched people dance, listened to a lot of bullshit about rope horses, felt the party going on around me. The band started "The Auctioneer's Song."

"Do you want to dance?" Lonny asked me.

I smiled and took his hand, and we walked out on the dance floor. Started the smooth in-and-out step, moving with the music. Lonny twirled me and spun me and swung me. I had glimpses of his face, flashes of his eyes laughing with pleasure. Back and forth, in and out, always in time. The lights and faces of the barroom blended with the music, and there was only the pure fun of this one thing and Lonny's eyes, as alive and wholehearted as any eyes in the world.

The band finished "The Auctioneer's Song" in the classic sped-up whirl, and Lonny and I danced it out, swinging and stepping at top speed. When it ended with the final "Sold that hog for a twenty-dollar bill," he bent me back over his leg and I gave myself to the move, my body arching, my hair almost brushing the floor. Lonny lifted me up with the last chord and looked into my face, smiling, his hands around my waist, then hugged me.

It was the most natural thing in the world, a friendly hug, but it hit me like a sledgehammer. His body fit mine intimately, automatically, my arms wrapped easily around his shoulders, my breasts pressed against his chest. A rush of desire crashed through me like a wave.

Lonny looked me in the eyes. I could smell his scent, as individual as personality. Our eyes stayed steady. I couldn't hide the hunger in mine. Lonny's expression was unreadable.

He took his hands off my waist. Put one arm casually around my shoulders. Walked me off the floor. I stopped him before we reached the bar. "Lonny," I said.

He looked at me.

"Lonny, the answer is yes."

"But you said . . . ," he began carefully.

"That was then; this is now. Let's go home."

He didn't need telling twice. I said good-bye to Lisa and told her I'd be back in the morning, and Lonny and I were out the door. Less than an hour later we were in his bed.

It felt great, better than I could have imagined. My body flared with longing and pleasure; each touch, from the first kiss to the last surge, seemed electrically charged. When at last we lay next to each other, naked and wet, exhausted and complete, Lonny said gently, "I love you."

"I love you, too," I murmured into his shoulder.

"So where does it take us?" he asked.

"I don't know. Isn't this enough for now?"

"For now," he agreed. A minute later, he was asleep.

NINETEEN

The rigs started pulling into Glen's parking lot at eight the next morning. Everyone looked a little more sullen and a lot less awake than they had yesterday.

"I think these guys are victims of overparty." Lisa smiled at me as she said it. We were saddling our horses out at the barn, and she, at least, looked wide awake.

"Where's Tim?" I asked.

"Who knows. I left the bar when Dad did. Tim stayed." Lisa looked over my shoulder and laughed. "There he is now. I wonder who he went home with."

Tim drove Sixball up to the barn and parked right in front of us. We both watched him get out. He looked a little crumpled and a lot worse for wear, but he ambled toward us unhurriedly, grinning his lazy grin. "Huh?" he said.

"Huh?" Lisa answered him back. "Rough night?"

Tim shrugged. "No rougher than usual."

He headed out to the corral to catch Roany.

"I guess he isn't going to tell us where he was," Lisa said. She didn't sound particularly worried about it.

I scanned the arriving crowd, noting that Charles Domini

was, once again, accompanying Pat, though he wasn't roping. No sign of Sonny Santos anywhere, unless he was hiding in some camper.

"The same folks as yesterday, it looks like?" I said inquiringly at Lisa.

"Except . . ." She pointed.

Sitting at one of the picnic tables under the big oak were Susan Slater and her companion. A closer inspection revealed their protest signs lying at their feet.

"They weren't here yesterday," I commented.

"And everything went just fine," Lisa said significantly. "Keep an eye on them, Gail."

I shook my head at her. "You keep a good eye on Glen. That's what counts. I'm a long way from convinced that Susan's responsible for your accidents."

Lisa didn't say a word, just swung on Chester and rode off. I climbed on Gunner and followed her.

The roping continued as planned. The two brothers from Watsonville missed their first steer, as I'd half-suspected they would. Sitting second was too much pressure at their level of experience. Then Lonny missed the second steer for Wes Goodwin and put the two of them out. Lonny was pretty unhappy about it, which I more than understood. He had drawn a difficult steer, but still . . . Wes was probably the best heeler in the whole arena. It seemed criminal to miss for him.

Tim and Billy Walsh kept roping cleanly and went to the lead, while Lisa and I managed to catch everything we drew and maintained our position on the average, despite the fact that we both had one eye on Glen the whole time. We were sitting third at two o'clock, when the show moved up the road to eat barbecue at Glen's. Afterward we'd rope the last steer, with the top teams competing for trophy saddles and all the money.

Sitting in a chair on Glen's patio, I asked Lisa, "So do you get nervous when you have to make a high team run?"

She shook her head. "No, I don't get scared anymore. The

only way I can enjoy going roping is not to care if I win or lose and just go out there and do the best I can. I take the pressure off myself."

I nodded. My own adjustment to competitive team roping was similar. I was not inclined to the sort of mental torture some ropers put themselves through; I had once told a particularly uptight partner, "It's not that big of a deal for God's sake. It's just a roping, not a religion." Judging by his expression, he thought that particular heresy ought to be punished by burning at the stake, at the very least.

Lisa smiled. "Tim's the one who's intense."

We both watched Tim, who was flirting with a blond girl I'd never seen before. Tim had always been an intense competitor, in odd contrast to his lazy, relaxed attitude about life in general. He wanted to win, and pressure seemed to act on him like a tonic; it only added to his focused intensity. Being high team out wouldn't bother Tim at all.

I remembered Bret had once told me that Tim's childhood dream was to become a professional horse trainer. I thought it too bad he'd never pursued it. Tim might have been a great showman.

I leaned back in my chair a little and looked out across Glen's wide green lawn. The oak trees on the other side threw dark shadows on the smooth grass. There was a barbecue pit in the middle, with Glen tending the steaks. The lawn and patio were dotted with people, standing, sitting, all talking. I took a long swallow of chilled chardonnay—a nice change from the inevitable beer—and thought that the dusty, rough-looking ropers seemed a little out of place on the brick patio, the big lawn. A crowd of martini-drinking golfers wearing slacks or shorts would have looked more appropriate.

I watched Joyce setting out bowls of salad on a picnic table. She was dressed in black, which was striking with the silver-ash hair, but which made her face look older, coarser. Her eyes drifted around the crowd, and I wondered if she was picturing

161

golfers, stockbrokers, suntanned men in white linen, men who owned yachts, or, if they had to have horses, polo ponies. You couldn't tell. Her flat, glassy blue eyes rested on me for a second and then moved on. She was looking at Pat Domini.

Pat stood next to Charles, who was talking loudly to a group of men. She seemed poised and confident in her dusty jeans—at home with the ropers around her. Charles looked like an arrogant bore, at least to me. I wondered, as I had before, what Pat had ever seen in him.

Lisa broke into my thoughts. "Do you have any more of an idea who's trying to get at Dad?"

She asked the question casually, but I wasn't fooled. I knew that she, like me, remained intensely aware of the unknown threat that hung over Glen.

Lisa and I sat more or less by ourselves in one corner of the patio, up against the wall of the house. No one was around us; Lonny had gone over to talk to Wes Goodwin, apologizing once again for the missed steer, no doubt. I watched Lisa's face. "Who do you think is doing it?" I asked her.

"Sonny," she said slowly. "I guess. If it isn't that damn Susan. Did you see her?"

"I saw her."

Susan and her friend had waved their signs all morning and attempted to distribute flyers to the crowd. They were hindered by the fact that virtually everyone there was either a roper or related to one; there were few spectators open to the stated mission of the flyer: "Stop Rodeo Cruelty!"

I had taken one from Susan's friend and read it. It seemed basically uninformed and inflammatory to me; I thought that Susan and company were lucky that the ropers were inclined to avoid them, rather than argue with them.

"Susan's not doing anything wrong," I said slowly. "She's just standing up for her beliefs. I may not agree with her entirely, but I suspect she's honest enough."

"You don't think she's the stalker, do you?" Lisa asked.

"It doesn't really fit."

"What fits, then?"

I looked out across the lawn. Wondered what to tell her. "I don't know yet," I said finally. "I'm waiting."

"Waiting for what?"

"For something else to happen."

Lisa's eyes snapped back to mine. "Shit, Gail. The next thing could kill him."

"What else is there to do?" I demanded. "What we need is some kind of definite proof—some evidence that will connect a person to the 'accidents.' Then we can either take it to the cops or convince Glen to do something."

Lisa's lips tightened. "I think Dad's in real danger."

"I'm afraid so. But I'm not sure what we can usefully do besides warn him, which we've done, and watch him. We could tell the police right now, but I don't think they'd do anything at this point, and Glen would probably shoot us."

Lisa gave a faint smile. "Agreed. But I wish you'd tell me what you're thinking."

"I will." We looked at each other. "As soon as I have one single scrap of evidence."

Tim chose that moment to walk up and sit down. "I've come to put some pressure on Lisa so she'll miss your steer," he said cheerfully.

Lisa wrenched herself away from our conversation with an obvious effort. She gave me a warning glance, then said, "Not likely, buddy. You're high team out, remember? All the pressure's on you."

It was clear that Lisa was as reluctant to discuss the threat to Glen in front of Tim as I was. They were talking about roping now. I didn't listen. I was watching people. Watching Charles Domini talking loudly and aggressively to Wes Goodwin. Watching Al Borba standing silently in a group of men, drink in hand. Watching eyes.

Janey Borba walked across the lawn in another skintight

T-shirt and jeans. I saw Tim's eyes lock onto her. Janey was headed for the makeshift bar on the other end of the patio. Tim got up quickly. "Think I'll go fix Janey a drink," he drawled, and went off in her direction.

I watched Joyce pass a tray of crackers and cheese to a group of ropers a little way away from us. The thought that had been in my mind surfaced, and I turned back to Lisa. "Does Tim ever talk about getting a job or moving out or anything?"

Lisa looked startled. "You mean leaving the ranch?"

"Yeah," I agreed. "Leaving the ranch."

Lisa thought about it. "Not in a long time. He used to talk about going to work for Will George or one of the other big-time cow-horse trainers. Tim could do it, too. He's really talented with a horse."

"Why doesn't he?"

"He's lazy, I guess. He'd rather lie around all day and watch TV. Dad doesn't make him work. Tim pretty much does whatever he wants to do. It's an easy life."

"But frustrating, don't you think?"

Lisa didn't answer.

Lonny bore down on us, smiling into my eyes, bad humor apparently forgotten.

"Wes forgive you?" I teased.

"Oh, yeah. I just haven't forgiven myself." Lonny grinned sheepishly, and I had the sudden impulse to put my arms around him and kiss him long and hard, right in front of everybody.

He must have guessed something of my thought, because his smile widened and he reached for my hand. "You can cheer me up later," he said.

Lisa shook her head at the two of us. "I'm going to get something to eat."

We had steak for dinner. Steak and chili beans and potato salad and macaroni salad and green salad and strawberries and garlic bread. With brownies and chocolate chip cookies and homemade vanilla ice cream for dessert. By the time everybody was done eating, the sun was resting just above the bay, filling the air with the mellow golden light of evening. There was a slow, steady drift of people out to the pickup trucks and down to the arena.

I sat on Gunner next to the arena fence and watched the horses lope around. Glen limped over and stood near me.

"Nice roping, Glen," I said. "Great barbecue."

He gave me a faint smile. "Got to do it," he said. "They expect it."

Lisa loped by and his smile broke free. For a second he looked like the Glen Bennett of my youth. "Boy, she can really rope, can't she?" he said.

I smiled back at him. "Yes, she can."

Tim pulled Roany up next to us. "Al wants to know if you're ready to start," he told his father.

"Sure we are." Glen's voice and face were wooden again.

Tim trotted Roany back across the arena, and in a minute we could hear Al's voice. "Let's rope!"

I stood by the fence and watched the ropers file out to stand behind the chutes. The sun was down below the hills, and the peculiar deep stillness of evening hovered just behind the noise and bustle of the roping arena. The sky to the west was blue-green, peacock blue, aquamarine. Let's rope, I thought. The call to the faithful.

Glen turned toward me. For a minute I expected him to say something, answer the question I hadn't asked. He was as much of a past as I had. I'd admired that stoic, strong presence ever since I could remember. Say something, Glen, I thought. Is it enough, what you are? Would you change if you could? And why does someone hate you?

Our eyes met. I thought he must have heard me, the questions were so loud in my own mind. But the square, strong face was as quiet and sure as ever, the eyes steady, the voice even. "I guess I better go turn the lights on so you guys can see to rope," he said.

I watched him turn and limp away.

In a minute the lights came on, adding their electric daylight to what was left of the real thing. Al was bellowing at the top of his lungs, yelling out the order. The teams would go in reverse; Tim and Billy Walsh, as high team, would be the last to go. Lisa and I were third to last.

The first team came flashing out under the lights and charged down the arena, throwing dirt clods in the air. They were chasing a brindle steer who could really run. The header never caught up and just pitched his rope at the steer in a no-hope shot somewhere near the end of the arena.

Lonny rode up to me and parked Burt near the fence. "I'd say he got outrun."

I nodded. "That gray horse doesn't have enough speed to be a real good contest horse."

"No," Lonny agreed. "He's pretty honest, though. That was a tough steer."

I smiled. This was part of it, this endless discussion of horses, this shared assumption that the equine species was infinitely interesting. We watched the next couple of teams go.

It was getting darker. I scanned the crowd, looking for anything that wasn't right. I could see the white protest signs waving gently about halfway down the arena. Susan and friend were still here, it appeared. They certainly hadn't been invited to the barbecue.

Lisa rode up next to me. Her eyes met mine—a quick, involuntary glance. Immediately we both looked for Glen. I was relieved to see him located prominently by the chutes, helping Al load the cattle and turn them out.

"So what do you think?" I asked Lisa.

Her face was tense; she glanced at Lonny, then flashed me a brief smile that reminded me for a split second of her father. "I think we're going to win this roping," she said.

166

"No all-girl team's ever won the Rancher's Days roping."
Tim's voice. He'd ridden up on his sister's side.

"I'll bet you twenty dollars this all-girl team does." Lisa
sounded a lot more confident than I felt.

Tim grinned. "Good luck, big sister. You're gonna need it."

The sky grew steadily darker. Above the glare of the electric
lights it appeared almost black, with a dark blue band glowing
over the western hills.

Al was calling out the last ten teams. I trotted Gunner around
to loosen him up. Al yelled, "Gail and Lisa, get ready."

Lisa smiled at me. "Here goes," she said.

The roping wasn't shaping up to be too tough. There was
only one good time posted among the teams that had already
gone. Lisa and I had twelve seconds to go to the lead. After that
it depended on what Mark Brown and Travis Gunhart, who
were the second high team, and Tim and Billy Walsh could do
with their steers.

Lisa rode off toward the box, Chester walking relaxed, his
head down, his hindquarters shambling from side to side in a
loose, rocking gait. His eye was quiet and docile. That was how
some of the really good ones were. They'd plod into the box like
plow horses and then turn around and outrun anything in the
arena.

I rode Gunner into the header's box, feeling my heart pound.
This was it. Backing Gunner into the corner, I gathered him up
and felt him come to instant readiness, muscles bunched, body
half-crouched. For a second everything stood still, the horses
frozen in the moment of waiting, tense and ready. Then I nodded for the steer and the still moment dissolved itself into speed
and motion.

We drew a pup, a little white-faced steer who didn't run
much, and I roped him neatly around the horns, turned him off,
and took him away perfectly. I could hardly believe I'd done it.

Lisa came in hard after the steer, rope whirling, and threw. It
was a good loop, and the steer's back feet went into it. She

pulled the rope tight, dallied around her saddle horn, and I swung Gunner around to face. The flagman dropped the flag. My whole body relaxed. The timers called out an eight-second time and announced that Lisa and I were winning the roping.

Tim grinned at us as Lisa and I rode back up the arena together. "How 'bout that?" he called to his sister and me. He was tightening the cinch on Roany, getting ready for his run.

"It's all up to you now," Lisa teased him.

I got off Gunner and loosened his cinch, then tied him to the fence. Lonny walked up and put an arm around my shoulders. "You did great," he told me. "Your horse worked perfectly."

I patted Gunner's neck, still too stunned to speak.

Glen limped toward us. "Good job," he said impartially to Lisa and me.

The words were still in his mouth when there was a sudden ominous electric crackle. The big arena lights flickered and then went out. It was like a curtain coming down. Only a couple of smaller lights still glowed by the chutes. We all looked at each other in the semidarkness.

"God damn it," Glen said. "The girls in the timer's shack must have turned on the heater. They should know better than that. Any time we turn that heater on when the arena lights are on it overloads the whole system. Hell."

He jerked a flashlight out of the pocket of his jacket and hobbled toward the timer's shack.

"Does he need any help?" I asked Tim and Lisa.

"Nah," Tim said. "He's the only one who knows how this arena works. These lights do this all the time."

I started after him anyway, propelled more by a desire to keep an eye on him than anything else. I saw his flashlight go bobbing into the timer's shack, and I could hear his voice raised inside, half-teasing, half-annoyed: "Now just what do you girls think you're doing, running that heater when I've got the arena lights on? You all know that overloads the system."

Lots of giggles and disclaimers. I peered in the door. Glen

was flicking switches by flashlight. Janey Borba, Pat Domini, a woman I didn't know, and Joyce stood there watching him. The stranger woman was laughing and denying that any of them had turned the heater on.

Glen stepped back out and hopped down the arena on his crutches. Most of the crowd were sitting quietly on their horses in the half-dark, waiting for things to get started again. I followed Glen. He moved at a surprisingly rapid pace for a man on crutches. I kept my antennae out for trouble, but no one else seemed to be trailing Glen—only me.

Glen stopped by a power pole; I could see the fuse box partway up it. Glen cursed softly; he appeared to be fumbling in the box by flashlight. He seemed to find what he wanted, and I heard a click.

There was a brief yellow glow from the lights, but in the same instant an electric crackle and an arcing green-white flash lit the fuse box, illuminating the black silhouette of Glen's stiffened body for the split second before everything went dark again.

Then Glen's body was falling and I was running to him and he was lying on the ground, ominously still. Somebody was with me and we rolled Glen on his back and I saw that the somebody was Lisa. Her face was desperate. I took one close look at Glen and said, "Quick, you work on his heart. I'll breathe into him."

I pinched Glen's nose and opened his mouth, tilted his chin back. Took a deep breath. Pressed my mouth over his and blew my breath into him. When I lifted my head, I could see Lisa pumping his chest. *One one thousand, two one thousand . . .* I said a quick, silent prayer of thanks for the CPR lessons that Lisa and I had taken while we were in high school.

I could hear people yelling around me with part of my mind, but most of me was quiet and focused. There was only Glen's face and the stubble of rough whiskers on his jaw. Come on, Glen, I thought. Come on.

I couldn't tell how long we worked on Glen. It seemed like

hours. Eventually there was a red light flashing and Lisa and I were pulled away as others took over. Glen was still alive, they said. They loaded him in an ambulance on a stretcher, and Joyce got in with him. Tim and Lisa got in Tim's truck and followed the ambulance. Lonny had his arm around my shoulders as we watched the sad little entourage pull out.

After they were gone, people huddled together. The roping was over; Al was turning the cattle out. No one seemed very concerned that the fate of the saddles was undecided. The real drama of Glen's near-death was the only topic of discussion. The ropers wanted to talk, to speculate, to reassure each other.

"Jesus, Gail, what happened?" Lonny had shepherded me away from the group and was plying me with coffee.

"I don't know." I said it between sips and shudders; the night had grown chilly, and my hands were shaking. Shock, not cold. "I shouldn't have waited," I said numbly.

"What do you mean?" Lonny was clearly puzzled. "You saved his life. What more could you do?"

"I don't know," I said again. "But I should have done something." I turned to Lonny. "Could you do me a favor?"

"Sure."

"Unsaddle my horse. Unsaddle the Bennetts' horses, too. I need to look around for a minute."

"All right." Lonny sounded doubtful, but he moved off.

I walked over to the fuse box. I wasn't exactly sure what I was looking for, but what I found puzzled me more than ever. There were no fuses anywhere. There was no fuse in the spot where a fuse was supposed to be, only an empty bracket. There were no spare fuses on the small shelf at the bottom of the fuse box. I looked carefully, using the flashlight that had fallen when Glen dropped. No fuses on the ground below or beside the box, either.

Then I walked back to the timer's shack. It was quiet and empty; everybody was outside talking. I looked at the main breaker switch, the switch I assumed Glen had flipped off when

170

he was in there earlier. I stared at it a long time. It was in the off position. There was no way, with the switch in that position, that Glen could have electrocuted himself. The thing was physically impossible.

I walked out of the timer's shack slowly, not paying any attention to what was going on around me, and almost ran into Janey Borba, who was walking in. She spooked like a startled horse. It only took her a half-second to lose the startled look and resume her usual unfriendly expression.

"What are you doing in here?" she demanded. She didn't acknowledge by word or tone that she had any idea who I was, though I assumed she knew.

"I'm not sure," I told her truthfully.

I could feel her looking after me as I walked away.

TWENTY

I spent another hour at the barn, helping Lonny unsaddle and feed the Bennetts' horses, avoiding people who wanted to pat me on the back as gracefully as I could. By the time we were done, almost everybody had gone home.

"Could you take me up to Lisa's?" I asked Lonny. "I'm going to wait there until she gets home. If . . ." I didn't want to put it into words. "She might need a friend," I finished.

"Do you want me to stay with you?"

"No, better not. Somebody's got to feed our horses at your place."

"I could feed the horses and come back."

"That's OK." I spotted Glen's pickup sitting by the barn." I can drive Glen's truck up to Lisa's. I'll call you if I need you."

Lonny looked like he wanted to argue, but after a glance at my face he gave in. "Whatever you say. Call me if anything seems wrong."

"I will."

I walked over to Glen's truck and got in. The keys were in the ignition. Glen always left them there. Nobody questioned my right to the truck. Al and Janey had vanished into their mobile home; virtually everyone else was gone, too.

I drove up the road to Lisa's house with my mind racing. I had ideas, but they wouldn't come together. A little doe jumped into the path of the headlights and out again. I barely noticed her.

When I drove down into the valley I was greeted by the angry racket of dogs barking. The headlights showed them plainly, jumping and snarling inside the picket fence. I stared through the windshield at the pointed faces with the big bat ears. They seemed to have an awful lot of teeth.

I sighed. Parked the truck and got out in one motion. Walked toward the yard like I owned it. Besides a brisk, "Shut up, you guys," I ignored the dogs. They were still barking and growling when I opened the gate and walked inside the fence. "Good dogs," I said casually and hoped that everything I'd heard about dogs being able to sense fear was a lie.

They sniffed my jeans, muttering suspiciously. I gave them a minute and then headed for the door. They followed me. I heard the snick of teeth on the air behind my heels, but they didn't bite me.

Lisa had left the door unlocked. I opened it and went in, shutting the dogs outside. At the sound of the latch the big orange cat came galloping out from the back of the house, meowing loudly.

"What's the matter with you?" I demanded.

He meowed louder and rubbed against my ankles, then stood on his back legs and put his front paws on my thigh. He looked at me steadily and reached out a paw to grab my hand. I jerked it back, startled. "Dammit, Zip," I snapped at him.

He flattened his ears for a second but held his ground, staring intently up into my face. He gave me a long, soulful meow.

"What do you want?" I asked him. "Are you hungry?"

I walked toward the kitchen and he ran along beside me, chirping excitedly. When I stepped into the room he jumped on

174

the counter and gave a short, sharp, *Murrrt.* It sounded like an order.

Sure enough, there was a dish on the counter. It was empty. I looked in the cupboard under the counter, produced a paper bag full of dry cat food, and poured out a little dinner. Zip was ecstatic. He was also quiet. Relieved, I went to the refrigerator and got myself a glass of wine.

I walked back into the living room and sat down on the couch. Put my feet up on a battered coffee table and stared into space. The rough pine-planked walls were hung with a couple of framed Charles Russell prints. The one facing me was called *Broncos for Breakfast.* It showed a bucking horse tearing up a trail camp while the crew looked on. I'd seen it many times. I stared at it now for an hour, as if it held the answer. As if the face of Glen's killer could be found around that campfire.

The stalker had moved on to murder. Or attempted murder, anyway. God willing, Glen was still alive. I thought of calling the hospital and decided not to. Lisa would come home eventually. When she did, I'd hear the news, whether good or bad.

I got up and went into the kitchen and made a pot of coffee. Poured myself a cup and sat down to stare some more. Two more cups of coffee later, I had the ghost of an idea.

The house seemed empty and quiet. I built a fire in the wood-stove; the air was cold enough for the warmth to be inviting. I left the stove door open and watched the flames flicker. It gave me something to stare at.

It was well past midnight when I heard the sound of a truck coming down the hill. The dogs heard it, too. They began to bark in short, high, excited tones. Welcoming barks. Lisa was home.

I felt anxiety knot itself in my stomach. Let him be alive, I thought fiercely. Death was too final. Let him be alive.

There was Lisa's step on the porch and the door opened and Lisa and the dogs came in together. The dogs bustled around, sniffing happily and wagging their bobbed tails. Lisa looked exhausted. She didn't seem surprised to see me; she barely seemed to notice me. There were smudged shadows under her eyes, and her expression was vacant. I took a step toward her and held out my arms slightly, looked a careful question in her direction.

She met my eyes. "He's alive," she said simply. She slumped down on the couch, and I sat down next to her and put an arm around her shoulders. "He's off the machines, but he's still unconscious," she said. "They say he'll live. They don't know if there's any brain damage."

I sighed in relief. At least Glen was alive. "Where's Tim?" I asked.

"He's still at the hospital. He said he was going to stay with Dad." Lisa stared straight ahead. "I just couldn't sit there in that waiting room anymore, not knowing. Tim said he'd call if anything happened."

"I'm sorry, Lisa," I said. It sounded inadequate. "I don't know what to say. I'm sorry this happened to Glen. That I didn't stop it."

Lisa shook her head. "We went over it together, Gail. It's my fault as much as yours. What could we have done?"

"I'm not sure. Confronted all the different people I suspected, maybe."

Lisa sagged farther down into the couch. "I can't face it," she whispered.

I wondered if she, like me, had suspicions that were almost too much to bear. I started to open my mouth, but she put a hand on my arm.

"Please. I can't talk about it. Not now. It's just been too much. Tell me tomorrow. Right now I just want to go to sleep. Will you stay here?"

"Sure."

"Sleep in my spare room. There's clean sheets on the bed." Lisa waved a hand at a door. "Thanks, Gail. Again. For everything." And she got up and left the room.

I walked through the door into a room like a large cupboard; the single bed filled most of it. It appeared to be a section of porch enclosed as an extra room for a child. The roof sloped at a steep angle to the one small window; no adult could have stood upright where it was lowest. Walls and ceiling were all paneled in rough, knotty wood. The little room was curiously reassuring and cozy, like a boat or the loft of a cabin. The narrow bed had a soft, brown patchwork quilt over it and clean-smelling sheets.

I stood on a scrap of woven rug that covered the tiny bit of open floor space and stripped off my shirt and jeans, dropping them where they happened to fall. Then I turned off the light, crawled into the bed, and fell unexpectedly and instantly asleep.

TWENTY-ONE

The phone woke me at dawn. Its shrill, persistent ring lifted my mind to consciousness, and I stared at the wall of Lisa's spare bedroom in momentary disorientation. The sight of Zip lying by my feet and purring loudly brought me back to where I was.

I got up and put my clothes on and walked into the kitchen. There was coffee in the pot on the stove, and Lisa was getting ready to leave. She handed me a cup and said, "They think he's waking up. Tim just called. I'm going to the hospital."

"OK," I said, taking my coffee. She'd showered and changed her clothes, I noticed, but the dark shadows under her eyes were even more pronounced than they'd been the night before. She clearly wanted to be out the door, and I decided that discussion of any type would have to wait until she'd seen how Glen was doing.

"Go ahead and go," I told her. "Let me know how he is."

"You'll be here?"

"I won't leave the ranch," I promised.

"I'll call you when I know something," she said. "Thanks again."

She gave me a thin smile, set her coffee cup down on the table, and was out the door. I walked to the window and watched her get in the truck and drive off, her movements as definite and competent as always. She took the red dog with her. I could see Rita's head through the truck window, the sharp ears flattened out wide, mouth parted in a riding-on-the-seat grin.

I called the clinic and told them I had a family emergency and wouldn't be in today. Then I called Lonny and told him what was happening, reassured him I was fine. Then I opened the door. Joey gave me his usual don't-bother-me look, but he got up and walked over to me when I called him. "Good dog," I said. "You want to come in?"

I held the door open for him. He wouldn't look at me, but he walked into the house and lay down by the couch. I smiled. Got myself another cup of coffee and sat down on the couch, stretching my legs out next to the dog. A few minutes later, I could feel him imperceptibly leaning against my ankles—a gentle, warm pressure.

Staring out Lisa's east-facing window at another brilliant morning, I wondered what to do. Or what to do first. The sunlight made cheerful golden patches on the wooden floor, and I was tempted just to sit here. But it wouldn't work.

When I left the house an hour later, I shut the dog in the yard again. He gave me a hopeful look as I walked out the gate. "You stay here," I told him. "I'll be back."

I drove down to the barn slowly. Glen's house looked deserted—no vehicles in evidence. Al's truck was parked squarely in front of his mobile home; Janey's red sports car was gone. I parked Glen's truck in front of the barn, where Glen usually left it, and got out.

The air was bright and chilly and sharp with the spicy smell of bay leaves. All the horses were fed; everybody's head was down, eating. No people in sight anywhere. I shot a glance across Lone Oak Road to the parking lot of the Saddlerack. No cars or trucks that I could see. I shrugged. Started walking back up the hill to Glen's.

The driveway and the garage were still empty at the big house. I went in through the back door. It was unlocked; it always was.

The house seemed very quiet. I walked as silently as I could, but even on the carpet I could hear the soft sounds of my footsteps. I walked down a long hall lined with glass-fronted cases full of china plates to the door at the end. I hesitated a moment, then opened the door and went in.

Glen and Joyce's bedroom was big, with a high ceiling, and like the living room gave an impression of emptiness. The carpet was a smooth, deep peach. There were items of furniture here and there—a dresser with a large mirror and a row of lights, a couple of chairs. There was a walk-in closet in the corner. But for all practical purposes, there was only one thing in the room; it caught and held all the attention.

In the center of the carpet stood a huge brass bed. Bright and shiny, its gaudy lines loud against the peach carpet, it was swathed in yards and yards of snow white fabric worked out in eyelet lace. It had skirts and flounces and ruffles and cushions and bows, all neatly fluffed up and unwrinkled.

I stood and stared around the empty room for quite a while. There was a row of French doors that led out onto the patio, all shut down tight, draped in the same white lacy fabric as the bed. Some soft daylight filtered in. I took a couple of steps forward. Went into the closet.

Racks of brightly colored women's clothes, rows of high-heeled shoes and dressy boots. And Glen's scuffed work boots and his beat-up slippers. Some plain long-sleeved men's shirts, a neat stack of Wrangler jeans on a dresser.

I stood in the middle of the closet, still unable to bring myself to do what I had come here to do. I couldn't really believe I was actually standing here. What I was about to attempt was so foreign to me that I had a hard time even contemplating it.

181

Only the memory of Glen's still, gray face made it seem possible, even necessary.

Come on, I told myself. Just do it, Gail. But I still stood like a statue.

I wasn't a cop or a private eye; I was a veterinarian. I didn't feel I had any right to be here. In fact, I felt ridiculously, stupidly, out of line. Do you want him to die? my mind demanded. If you don't, then do something.

I started opening the drawers of the dresser. Found the dirty clothes and looked through them, keeping one ear cautiously alert for any noise outside the bedroom. I didn't hear anything. Didn't find anything, either.

On the floor beside the dresser was a dusty black pair of women's boots. Behind them, against the wall, was a black purse and a black leather jacket. I picked up the jacket and felt in the pockets—nothing. I picked up the purse and looked through it. Lipstick, sunglasses, a comb, a little mirror. And a smooth, hard, cylindrical object. I brought it up and out of the purse. Held it in my hand and looked at it closely. It was plain enough in the pale light that came through the curtained windows. I just stood there looking at it.

I heard a tiny creak and started, dropping the purse back on the floor and shoving the thing I held into my jeans pocket. Maybe a guilty conscience sharpened my nerves, but as I stepped out of the closet and looked toward the doorway of the bedroom, I half-expected what I saw. Joyce walked quietly from the hallway into the room, moving with unnerving silence. In her hand she held a gun.

Whoever she expected, it wasn't me. When her eyes met mine, she almost jumped. "Gail," she said sharply, "what are you doing here?"

I hadn't heard her coming, I thought unhelpfully. I looked down and saw that she was barefoot, her feet pale and white against the peach carpet. No wonder, I thought, and, What am I going to say?

We stared at each other almost blankly, and various things went whirling through my mind and out again. It was time for a snap decision, and I wasn't sure which way to jump.

Joyce made up my mind for me. She lowered the gun. "What are you doing in my bedroom?" she said again, but the alarm in her voice was reduced to annoyance.

"Lisa sent me to get some clothes for Glen," I said, trying to cover my confusion. "I didn't think you were at home or I never would have come in here."

"I see." Her eyes were still flat and cold, but I thought she looked relieved. I glanced pointedly at the gun that was still in her hand.

She looked down at it, too, and then her oddly opaque-looking blue eyes moved back to my face. "I just got home. I heard someone moving around in here and thought it was a burglar," she said. "I took my shoes off and got out the gun." She smiled faintly. "I know how to use it."

That was true, I remembered. Joyce had been a very good shot when I was in high school. Glen had built her a private range up behind the house, and Lisa and I had watched her practicing. Self-defense, she had said, living out here on the ranch. Judging by her demeanor, she seemed prepared to use her talent.

She stared at me some more. I could only guess at the thoughts that were going through her mind, but I noticed she wasn't hurrying to put the gun away.

"Well," I said, trying a smile, "do you want to help me pick out some clothes for Glen?"

She thought about it and then put the gun back in her purse. It was a big white purse very like the big black purse I had been searching. Now that I thought about it, Joyce always seemed to have a big purse like that. Very handy for carrying a gun.

"Glen's still unconscious," she said without expression. "What does he need clothes for?"

"Tim called Lisa this morning," I said slowly. "They think he's waking up."

She looked surprised, I thought, not happy. But she walked into the closet and sorted out a shirt and jeans and underwear. "Here," she said. "You go ahead and take them. I'll be along in a little while."

I took the things from her and tried to keep any of what I felt from registering on my face. Her consternation seemed to be vanishing fast. She was composed and unruffled again, the eyes still flat and blank. I noticed that she was made-up, with carefully arranged hair, and that her light blue pants and top were unwrinkled. She didn't look as though she'd spent the night at the hospital. I wondered where she'd been.

"Thanks, Joyce," I said, as pleasantly as I could manage. "We'll see you later."

I heaved a deep sigh of relief once I was out of the house and walking away down the hill. Thanked God she hadn't asked me why I had walked and not driven. I didn't know what I could have said to that. The true answer—that I didn't want anyone to know I was there—would certainly not have done.

Glen's truck was still parked in front of the barn where I had left it. To my surprise, Lisa's truck was parked next to it. Lisa and Al and Janey were all standing in a little group in the barnyard, talking. I walked over and joined them.

Lisa smiled when she saw me, by which I judged that everything was all right. "How is he?" I asked.

"OK," she said. "He's awake and he seems normal. They say there's no brain damage. He's being a little strange, though. He doesn't remember what happened to him at all. Even though we told him he was electrocuted, he's acting like it was no big deal. He wants to go right home and get the rest of the cattle in so they can be shipped tomorrow the way he arranged." Lisa waved a hand at the holding pasture, which was heavily dotted with bovines. "They're all here except half a dozen that are still out in the back pasture. Dad seems obsessed with the idea he has to get home and get those gathered so everything can be shipped. The cattle trucks will be here tomorrow morning," she added.

I thought I understood. Glen wanted to feel that life was still normal, that nothing had changed. He needed the routines of the ranch to be important, needed to deny that there was a fundamental disaster at the heart of his world. I sighed inwardly. He wouldn't like what I would have to tell him.

"Those six steers are out on the far side of the back pasture," Lisa said. "They got away when we were gathering on Friday, and we didn't have time to go back for them." She looked at Al, Janey, and me doubtfully. "Could one of you guys go get them?"

Al and Janey were markedly silent. What the hell. "I'll go," I said. "Can I use Chester?"

"Of course," Lisa said gratefully. "I'm going back to the hospital. Tim's still there, trying to hold Dad down. If I can tell him the cattle are taken care of, maybe he'll sit still for the tests they want to do. If those go well, it's possible he can go home. He sure wants to." She glanced at the watch on her wrist. "I need to get going."

"Here's some clothes for Glen." I handed Lisa the bundle I was carrying and didn't explain anything more. There'll be time enough, I thought. That was a mistake.

Lisa took the clothes, talked to Al a little about shipping the cattle, and hurried away. I got back in Glen's truck and drove back to Lisa's house, collected Joey, and then went back to the barn and caught and saddled Chester. It was time to gather.

TWENTY-TWO

I rode along the dusty road to the back pasture. I had been there before, many times, helping Glen gather when I was a girl. This pasture was the largest field on the ranch—somewhere between five and six hundred acres—and was located, as the name suggests, at the back of the property. There was a dirt road that led from the barn to the back pasture; it wound down one side of a long gully full of redwood trees, then climbed a bare, empty hill to the pasture gate.

Chester marched readily along the road in a swinging walk, his ears flicking forward and back. Joey trotted behind. The rich scent of the redwoods filled the shadows; late-morning sunlight slanted through the branches in long shafts. It was a moment right off a postcard, and it barely registered on my mind.

I had too much else to think about. The main thing that emerged was that I needed to talk to Glen. Right away. Before something else happened.

I reached in my pocket and dug out the object I had found in Joyce's purse. It was a smooth copper bar about as big as a woman's little finger. About as big as a fuse, in fact. It was what

I had been looking for when I started to search, though I'd thought it unlikely I'd find it. A dummy fuse.

I stuffed it back into my pocket and stared blankly ahead of me. I saw and didn't see Chester's ears, red with black tips, his heavy, almost wavy black mane lying on the left side of his red neck. The redwoods slipped along beside me; a gray squirrel ran overhead, jumping from branch to branch. He was in another world—the safe, normal world I'd occupied before this last week. To be riding along trying to decide what to do about an attempted murder was unbelievable, unreal. Especially one involving Glen and Joyce, people I'd known since I was a kid. These things just didn't happen. I thought that I, like Glen, wouldn't mind returning to life as I'd known it.

The road descended down the side of the gully, getting steeper and steeper. Soon we would be at a little creek crossing, I remembered. Wrong. The road made a hard bend I didn't remember and showed me a brand-new bridge.

I stared at it in surprise. Chester stopped and stared, too. The bridge was a slender wooden ramp, with low rails, spanning the gully about twenty feet above the creek. I couldn't see the track of the old roadbed. As I recalled, it had descended in a sudden chute to the creek, a section that had been impassable for horse or vehicle in bad weather. No doubt this was why Glen had built the bridge. Apparently the bulldozing necessary to dig the footings had eliminated the previous roadbed.

Well, here goes, I thought. I clucked to Chester and bumped him gently with my heels. He took a step and stopped dead, his ears pointed sharply at the bridge. *Un-uh,* they said.

"Come on," I told him. "I know you've been over this before." I hoped it was true.

Chester wasn't buying it. He tried rooting all four feet to the ground; when I thumped steadily on his sides he took a hesitant step forward, then three fast steps backward. I thumped again and he jumped sideways. Not good.

A mere foot from his right front leg the bank dropped off

sharply to the creek twenty feet below. Rolling down this bank was a potentially lethal wreck. I presumed Chester had no more wish to do this than I did, but there was no accounting for taste. I also had no idea how much distaste Chester had for the bridge.

I considered my options while Chester stood rooted, staring at the horse-eating monster. If this had been Gunner, I would have kicked him sharply and told him to get on with it. But I knew Gunner, and Gunner knew and trusted me. Chester and I were strangers. I wasn't sure what he'd do if I insisted.

The hell with the cowboy ethic. I talked soothingly to Chester, patted his neck, and was able to climb off him without spooking him. Pulling the reins over his head, I led him to the bridge and walked out onto it.

Chester followed me docilely. As I'd more than half suspected, he'd obviously been over the bridge before, but probably always in a group of horses. No doubt an older horse had usually been in the lead. Chester was perfectly willing to follow me over the bridge, despite giving it several suspicious looks when he put his feet down on the echoing wooden ramp. Joey followed the two of us, unperturbed.

Once over, I remounted, and we wound our way up the far side of the gully and out into the open. The road followed a grassy slope toward the gate. Hills rolled away around us, empty and quiet. The wind blew the thin yellow strands of grass, and a buzzard circled in the distant blue. Silence washed over me like a physical wave. It was so damn quiet it was shocking.

I looked around, almost disoriented. The forest had been full of small noises—the whisper of the creek, rustles and creaks from the trees, the sounds of animals in the underbrush. Out here, in the open hills, there was only the thin sound of the wind. When it died—nothing. No distant traffic, no omnipresent background bustle. Nothing.

I realized I'd never been out here alone before. The force of the quiet emptiness had always been broken and diminished by the presence of other human beings. Alone, it was oddly over-powering. Almost disturbing.

I shook the feeling off and opened the gate to the back pasture. Rode Chester through it and shut it behind me. Wondered where the cattle were.

Lisa had said they were in the back, by the water hole, which made sense. If I was lucky, they were still there. Unfortunately, the water hole was at the far side of the field. I pushed Chester into a long trot and headed up the dusty road, Joey trotting behind me.

I rode for half an hour before I found the steers. They were where I expected them to be, grouped around a little puddle of a spring that made a tiny green island in the most desolate part of the ranch—an area called Jackass Pass. The hills here were so barren that in places they looked like a moonscape. The ground was chalky white, crumbling and dry. It was alien, un-friendly country to my eyes, though I supposed it had a certain stark beauty.

Counting heads, I ascertained I had six steers—the requisite number. All that remained was to get them back to the corrals near the gate. The nice thing about the back pasture was that, though big, it was roughly pie-shaped, narrowing steadily down-hill to the gate and the holding corrals. As cattle will almost al-ways go downhill when chased (horses go uphill), this made the pasture easy to gather, which was important if you were alone, as I was. The tricky part would be to keep the steers from hol-ing up in the brush, which was why I'd brought the dog.

I started the steers back toward the corrals. Joey made to charge after them, but I was prepared. I had a pocket full of pebbles. "Get back!" I hollered and hit him squarely in the ribs with a rock. He yipped in surprised and looked at me re-proachfully, but he did, indeed, fall in obediently behind my horse. A few more well-timed shots convinced him he should stay there unless I sent him.

I trailed the steers at a sedate pace, our assorted hooves raising puffs of dust in a small cloud. I coughed repeatedly and wondered why I'd ever wanted anything to do with horses and cattle.

Occasionally one of the steers, usually a high-headed brindle, would try and peel off into a patch of brush, in an attempt at escape. Fortunately, the brush was sparse on this part of the ranch, affording the cattle little cover. I sicced Joey on the brindle a couple of times, and the dog dove in enthusiastically, nipping and yapping, until the steer trotted back to the others, head and tail high. Two or three such lessons and the brindle gave up. After that, we all got along fine.

A black steer took over the lead, clopping steadily toward the corrals, seeming to know where he was going. Joey trailed behind the group, panting and happy. I relaxed and rode along in the rear, coughing intermittently.

There was plenty of time between coughs to think. I thought. None of the thoughts were pleasant. I kept adding up the events of the past week and wondering. There were a few things that just didn't fit, and I was at a loss to explain them. I had the unpleasant conviction that the things I didn't understand were vital.

We were almost back to the corrals. The cattle picked their way along a shallow dry creek bed, nosing at the occasional willows and cottonwoods. I turned my head to look for the dog, and a tree branch exploded next to me.

There was a split second of pure unreality; nothing in the world made any sense. Chips of wood stung my face, and a sharp crack echoed in my ears as Chester dove sideways with incredible frightened violence. Comprehension and adrenaline flooded into me in the same instant. I let go of the saddle horn in time to let the force of Chester's leap fling me off his back.

I landed rolling and flopped breathlessly and, I hoped, limply behind a boulder. Chester and the steers galloped off in a thundering herd. I didn't dare look for Joey. I lay perfectly still and listened to my heart thud.

That was a shot. My mind repeated it obsessively and use-lessly. Somebody was trying to kill me. A spine of rock dug into my leg where it was folded under me. I barely felt it. All I felt was intense, heart-stopping fear.

The boulder I lay behind was little better than no cover at all. Not to mention I wasn't exactly sure which direction the shot had come from. Near the corrals, I guessed.

I replayed the sharp crack that was still ringing in my ears. A rifle. The sniper could be a long way away, then, if he/she had a scope.

Joyce? I had never seen Joyce shoot a rifle before, only a pis-tol. That didn't mean she couldn't. Had Joyce discovered the dummy fuse was missing from her purse, learned from Lisa where I had gone, and marched out here to shoot me? There was a rack of deer rifles in the den at Glen's, I remembered.

Oh, shit. I was dead. The next shot would be coming any moment. If I hadn't turned my head, I'd be dead now. Holding my breath, I lay frozen.

I had no weapon, no way to protect myself. I could only hope that I would be taken for dead. If I were doing the shooting, I thought, I would be very wary. With a scope, I could hide in the trees back in the ravine and sight the rifle on my target up here. I wouldn't want to show myself, or shoot twice. One shot is often ignored; two might draw interest.

Lisa and Al and Janey knew I was out here. Any one of them, at any time, could come riding or driving up to check on me or help move the cattle. The road was passable for a pickup to the corrals, thanks to Glen's bridge. It wouldn't even take four-wheel drive. Joyce would not want to be seen. If I were found dead up here, she could not afford to have been in the area.

Joyce. Why hadn't I thought about it? Joyce had been suspi-cious of me. Of course the first thing she would do would be to look in her purse for the dummy fuse. When she found it gone, she would have known I'd taken it. Would have jumped to the conclusion that I knew. Joyce had to eliminate me.

I held my breath. The seconds passed with infinite slowness, but eventually they lengthened into minutes. Or I thought so, anyway. My heart pounded steadily, panic unrelieved. I could feel the rock digging into my leg, which was uncomfortably bent. I held still.

She would get away with it, I thought. No one would know Joyce had anything to do with Glen's accident; no one would know I suspected her. I hadn't told a soul. If I were dead, no one would imagine Joyce had a reason to kill me. Even if they found the dummy fuse in my pocket, it was doubtful anyone would put it together. And no one could know I had found the bar in Joyce's purse.

I had been incredibly, idiotically stupid. I had told Lonny I was in no danger, which was true, until Joyce discovered what I was doing. After that, I thought, Glen had been out of danger and I was the primary target.

The silence around me was all-encompassing. Echoes of the shot had died out of my ears. I could hear the thin wind now and then, an occasional rustle in the cottonwoods and willows. Some small thing, a lizard maybe, moved in the stones near my head.

I didn't dare twitch. If I was being watched through a scope, the tiniest movement might result in another shot. I lay still, not twitching.

My leg ached fiercely. How long, I wondered, would I need to lie like this? My eyes were open, staring straight ahead. I didn't dare blink or shift the angle of my vision. A scope could reveal those details from 200 yards away. My only hope was to lie perfectly still. Eventually Joyce, if it was Joyce, would have to either leave or come up here and see if I was dead.

Was it Joyce? It seemed as if it must be. Yet I wondered. My ears strained for any noise—a car engine, voices, the soft sounds of footsteps. The first two would be welcome, the third infinitely less so. Lisa might drive up here, looking for me. If I heard her coming I would know I was safe.

193

On the other hand, Joyce, if it was her, might decide to investigate. If she did, I told myself, I'd lie still till the last moment, then rush her. She would approach close enough to see if I was dead; she had to. She wouldn't risk firing a second shot for no good reason. I'd get a chance, I'd have to get a chance, to knock her down.

A sudden noisy rustle in the willows behind me sent my heart shooting up into my throat. The rustling continued, horribly loud in the silence. I lay frozen. Someone or something was moving through the willows.

More rustles. Getting closer. I lay still with every muscle tense. I could not make a mistake. I had to lie immobile until the person reached down to me, had to take that second to knock their legs out from under them. I had to.

More rustling, very close now. Silence. My heart pounded. She could be staring at me, getting ready to shoot. I wanted to jump up, break, and run, anything but lie still. That's how quail are killed, I told myself. Don't be a stupid quail. Hold still.

I ached with fear and held my breath. The brush rustled again, right next to me.

Something moved out where I could see it, something traveling into my line of vision. Gray speckles, furry, suddenly familiar—Joey. The relief was almost worse than the fear. I needed to do something. Yell at the dog. Cry. Instead I lay still, trying not to pee in my pants, feeling my heart beat in hysterical thuds. Jesus.

I kept on imitating a corpse. My leg was numb. I thought roughly an hour might have passed. It was probably about two o'clock in the afternoon. How long could I lie here? On the other hand, could I afford to move? The downside risk was pretty great.

Joey sniffed me a couple of times, puzzled and curious, and eventually lay down near me. I was glad of that. I thought he might bark if someone approached.

I longed for the sound of Lisa's voice, but the silence was

unrelenting. Why, oh, why had I gotten myself into this? Too late to cry, too late to back out. I lay still and ached all over, except for my leg, which I couldn't feel at all.

Please, dear God, I prayed fervently, unsure to whom I was praying but absolutely sure I needed help, please help me get through this. Help me survive.

TWENTY-THREE

A long, long time later the light began to die out of the sky. I lay where I had fallen, alternately throbbing and numb, trying to decide when to get up. Wait for dark, I told myself. You've waited this long. The rifle will be useless when it's dark.

I tried not to think about the pain, tried to relax and let the pain wash in and out, no more trouble than little waves along the beach. I watched the rocks in front of me as their outlines grew softer with the advance of evening.

The light was fairly dim and the air was getting cooler when I tried to straighten out my legs. I almost screamed. My right leg shrieked and throbbed. Oh, God. Oh, my God. I forgot about being shot as I shuddered and clenched my teeth.

Nothing happened. No shot. Nothing at all. My leg cramped in spasms that made me gasp. Inch by inch I straightened it out; slowly the devastating slashes of pain became drilling tingles. I moved in minuscule increments—my arms, my hands, my neck, my feet. A few mosquitoes whined in my ears. Crickets chirped. The light grew dimmer.

Eventually the pain subsided to a dull ache. Slowly I sat up. Nothing. Even more slowly (and extremely painfully) I got to my feet. Nothing happened. Joey walked up to me and wagged his bobbed tail. The sun was behind the western ridge, but there was still enough light in the sky that I could make out the dark shapes of trees and rocks, brushy and indistinct. Accurate shooting would be impossible. Time to go.

In reality, I thought, Joyce, or whoever, had probably been gone for hours. The thought shoved me forward, stumbling and hobbling, toward the gate. I needed to get to Glen.

Limping in the direction of the corrals, I was infinitely relieved to see Chester, peacefully cropping grass near the water trough. He'd broken his reins, but that appeared to be all the damage he'd sustained.

Knotting the reins hastily together, I led Chester to the corral fence to climb on him. I didn't think I could manage it from the ground.

Chester regarded me with a calm eye as I edged him up to the rails, all fear from the shot long forgotten. He stood like a perfect gentleman as I heaved myself up on him, my right leg cursing me in no uncertain terms. Between being folded up under me and pressed against a rock for over six hours, it was almost too stiff and sore to be usable.

"Come on." I clucked to the horse and dog indiscriminately as I opened the gate with one hand and let us out of the pasture. It was getting dark fast; the dirt road was a faintly lighter gray band running down the graying hillside.

Despite my aches, I urged Chester to a jouncy downhill trot, my fear driving me harder every second. Was Glen still alive?

The gully loomed up ahead, the shapes of the trees jet black against the charcoal sky. No sign of a moon. It had been a moonless evening, I remembered, when the lights had gone out at the roping. Damn.

Moonlight wouldn't have helped me in the canyon. It was claustrophobically dark under the redwoods; I couldn't see the road right in front of Chester's feet. Horses can see better in the dark than we can, I reminded myself. Chester can see the road. That's all that counts.

He seemed to be able to. He slowed from a trot to a long walk, but he kept rolling on, seeming sure of his footing, sure that he was going home. I almost fell off when he suddenly spooked and came to a jarring halt.

The bridge. Damn, damn, and damn. The frigging bridge. I couldn't see anything. I couldn't even see my hand if I held it up. The blackness was absolute. I had no idea if we stood on the edge of a precipitous drop. I couldn't see the bridge, but I knew it must be there.

My heart thumped steadily. I might as well have been killed by the sniper as go rolling down a cliff. I could get off, but I didn't know where I was. If I climbed off Chester, I might go over the bank. Chester could see, at least.

Gathering every atom of courage I possessed, I kicked the horse firmly. "Come on; let's go," I said out loud. "Let's go home."

Chester got my message. As a horse will do, he seemed to feel the urgency of my need, and, like the good ones, he came through. I could feel him take one, two, three cautious steps forward. He stopped; I could feel his front legs trembling. I clucked to him gently, and he took another step. I heard the hollow wooden clunks of his hooves coming down on the planking of the bridge.

Thunk, thunk, thunk. We were on it now, floating in the darkness above the gully. I tried not to picture the drop, tried not to remember how low the railing was. My right hand was locked tightly around the saddle horn; my left held the reins gently, trying to steady Chester and not disturb him. He kept walking, slowly and carefully. Thunk, thunk, thunk.

Abruptly the thunks stopped and Chester sped up. We were off the bridge and clambering uphill. I resisted the urge to ask for a trot. It was too dark and the bank was too steep.

We slid through the darkness, Chester moving effortlessly once we were up the hill. I clucked to him and he picked up the long trot, seeming confident. It was a strange feeling, trotting along when I couldn't see a thing. It required trust of an odd and unfamiliar sort, and I probably never would have tried it if I hadn't been driven by the need to hurry. Faster, my mind urged, faster.

Suddenly I could see lights ahead. After the unrelenting darkness they were an immeasurable relief. Civilization, help, safety. I could see that we were emerging from the canyon; the lights were on Glen's barn, which was lit up like a Christmas tree. I pulled Chester to a sudden halt.

My automatic reaction to those lights might not be smart. I was safe out here in the darkness. No one could see me; no one could shoot me. I was safely dead, in the mind of my assassin. Emerging into the light was another story.

Chester tossed his head and stamped his front feet anxiously. He could see the barn, too, and he wasn't pleased at being detained. "Come on," I could almost hear him saying. "You wanted to hurry; now we're here. Let's go home."

I patted his neck, which he ignored, flipping his nose up and down restlessly. What he wanted was to be turned loose in his pen with a flake of hay; being petted was of no interest. His agitation made it hard for me to think.

After a minute I got off of him, slowly and painfully, and unclipped his reins so he wouldn't step on them. Then I turned him loose. He trotted off, breaking immediately into a lope and heading for home.

I followed, limping, keeping to the verge of the road, staying behind convenient bushes. My eyes were glued to Chester. If someone was at the barn, waiting for me, they would surely come out to catch the horse. At the very least, their attention would be drawn to his obvious, noisy presence. No one would be looking for me out here in the shadows.

Something brushed against my leg, and I jumped and almost

shrieked. A second later the thought registered: It's just the dog. I reached down to pat his furry head, reassuring myself, and felt the warm, damp swipe of his tongue. "Good dog," I whispered.

I took a few more steps forward. Joey looked up at me with puzzled eyes. I could almost see him shrug. Then he turned away and trotted toward the barn, where Chester was traveling from corral to corral, greeting his friends. Joey was aiming for civilization. If I wanted to spend the rest of my life hiding out here in the brush, that was my business. He'd had enough.

I stopped behind a bay tree—the last useful cover before I reached the brilliantly lit square of bare ground around the big barn. I could see Chester; he'd come to rest at the hitching rail where he would normally be unsaddled and was nibbling on the alfalfa hay that had been spilled there. I could see no human beings.

Chester's arrival—all clattering hooves and shrill nickers, complete with loud answering neighs from the other horses— had produced no human activity of any sort. The barn was lit up and apparently deserted.

I pondered this. The barn must have been lit for my sake. It wasn't usually left like this. Why, then, was there no welcoming party; why, in fact, had there been no search party? It wasn't normal behavior to set out on what should have been a several-hour, at most, gather and not return till after dark. Lisa, at least, should have been worried about me. So where was she?

Not at the barn, as far as I could tell. I stood behind the bay tree for another few minutes, considering. Was this all some elaborate trap? Was the sniper waiting in the loft of the barn, rifle sighted on the road where it emerged into the light? The thought gave me chills.

I scanned the barn carefully but could see nothing out of place. No dead bodies in the barnyard, no rifle barrels emerging from windows or cracks in the wall. Of course, the odds that I could pick such a detail out from this distance were slim.

I could see Glen's truck, parked where I had left it. It didn't look as if it had been disturbed. As I watched, Joey marched up and lay down next to it, putting his chin on his front paws. He would wait there, I supposed, knowing that people eventually showed up to collect trucks.

Al's mobile home was illuminated by the front porch light, and the brown pickup and red Trans Am were parked in front of it. So why the hell wasn't Al out looking for me, or at least here at the barn waiting for me?

Impatience gathered in my muscles. Where was Glen? More important, where was Joyce? If I cut through the band of trees behind the barnyard, I would emerge onto the driveway that led up the hill to Glen's. I studied Chester. He looked content, his head down, nibbling. Chances were he'd be OK, for a little while. And I simply didn't dare risk an approach to that barn. I started off through the trees.

This was easier said than done. Once I moved away from the barn lights, the blackness seemed impenetrable. It was one thing to ride Chester through the dark, operating on blind trust; it was quite another to try and find my own way through it.

I stumbled over roots and walked into branches; I found myself pushing through tangles of brush I couldn't see, like invisible hands, pulling at me. It was creepy, at times downright terrifying. It had never occurred to me before how much I depended on my vision.

Glen's driveway couldn't be too far away. Or so I believed. Panic swept over me in a rush. I couldn't see anything; maybe I was going the wrong way. I was lost; I would never find my way out of this godforsaken forest.

Stop it, Gail. This is not the enchanted forest. It's just dark. Darkness is not evil; it is not full of bogeymen. It's just the absence of light. So you can't see. You're safe in the dark. No one can see you.

I stood still and took a deep breath. Concentrated on my relative safety. Then I began again to walk through the darkness toward Glen's driveway. Toward where I supposed Glen's driveway to be. I held my hands out in front of me to avoid running into branches and felt cautiously for each footfall. Even so, I tripped and ran into things on a fairly regular basis.

I cussed and swore softly as I crashed along and my shins got sorer, but I felt pretty sure the noise was unimportant. No one was likely to be hiding out here looking for me. As long as I avoided buildings and roads I was doubtless perfectly safe.

The thought reassured me, resigned me somewhat to the blackness. I pressed on, stumbling through the night for what seemed like miles. By my reckoning, it was a quarter-mile at most to Glen's driveway, but it sure seemed longer. My jeans and boots were soaked from stumbling into a little creek. I had bruises and scratches all over, and a wide assortment of brambles clung to me. I was out of breath when, in two crashing strides, the heavy blackness of the forest lifted into the soft darkness of a night sky sprinkled with stars. I was out in the open. Half a dozen more steps and I was on the road.

As my eyes were well accustomed to the darkness, I could see the pavement clearly. I had emerged onto it at the bottom of the hill; it ran up between rail fences; I could just make out the spiky silhouettes of red-hot poker plants. The road seemed empty and quiet. It also looked like wonderfully easy walking. I headed up it, keeping a sharp eye out for other vehicles, for movement of any kind.

I saw nothing, heard nothing. I pushed my aching muscles into a jog and pounded my way up the hill, gasping for breath. I almost tripped and fell on the cattle guard; my eyes were riveted to the lit windows of the big house.

Recovering myself, I stood stock-still. Glen's house was as bright as the barn had been. Floodlights illuminated the driveway and the patio. Most of the windows seemed to be glowing with light. Tim's truck, Lisa's truck, and Joyce's Cadillac were all parked conspicuously in the driveway.

I negotiated the cattle guard and crept out on the lawn. Staying in the cover of the oaks, I maneuvered my way around the house, peering in the windows as I went. No one in the living room or kitchen, though they were well lit. I moved on. No one in the den. Now I was opposite Glen's bedroom. And there they were.

I could see Glen, lying in the big brass bed, propped up by pillows. Joyce was sitting in an armchair by the door, wearing, it appeared, a blouse that was as white and frilly as the bedspread. Lisa and Tim were faced off in the middle of the room, both standing, apparently arguing. I heaved a deep sigh of relief. Glen was still alive. The Bennetts were behaving normally. I had a chance to save us all before somebody died.

What to do? Find out what they were saying, I decided. Fortunately, the lawn was narrow back here and the band of oak trees curved around it to brush up against the eaves of the house at the very back. The glaring floodlights that lit the patio didn't penetrate this far, either. I started to sneak around the lawn, trying to get closer to the French doors that appeared to be standing open with the filmy curtains drawn behind them. I could see through the curtains easily, but I was sure those inside could not see out.

Just walk across the lawn, Gail; they can't see you. That was the rational part of my mind. But the intuitive part wasn't about to leave cover. Nobody could see me to shoot me here in the trees. Out on the lawn, illuminated by the patio lights, I was a sitting duck.

I moved as noiselessly as I could; the oak grove border of the lawn was a great deal simpler to walk through than the wild forest. For one thing I could see, and for another it was neatly groomed, the only bush an occasional rhododendron or azalea—nice and tidy and easy to avoid. I crept up next to the French doors successfully. No one noticed me; no one shot at me.

I could hear Lisa, haranguing Tim in no uncertain terms. "We *have* to go look for Gail—something's happened to her; I know it has."

"She's probably down at the barn right now, unsaddling Chester." Tim.

"If she is, fine, but if she isn't, we need to go up there. Now. Come on, Tim."

"You go."

Lisa sounded truly astounded. "By myself, in the dark?"

"Take Al with you."

"For God's sake, Tim, what is the matter with you?"

"I'm staying here," Tim said flatly.

I couldn't see his face; his back was to the French doors. I could only guess at his motivation. I made a snap decision, one I was to wonder about a great deal, later. I walked into the room.

TWENTY-FOUR

Hi," I said. "I'm here." My eyes went rapidly from face to face. Joyce looked surprised, Lisa looked relieved and delighted, and neither Tim nor Glen registered any emotion that I could discern.

Glen was sitting up in the bed, propped with several white ruffled cushions. In contrast, his face appeared gray. He looked at least ten years older than when I'd seen him last.

Tim stood with his back to the French doors, his eyes watchful and noncommittal. He said nothing.

Joyce, on the other hand, rapidly shifted from surprise to displeasure. "What is going on here?" she demanded.

Lisa drowned her out. "Gail, where have you been? What happened to you? Tim and I just now brought Dad home from the hospital; I couldn't believe you weren't back. Where have you been?" she said again.

"Out getting shot at," I said.

For the first time, I looked directly at Glen, meeting his eyes. His face was wooden; he stared at me numbly, wearing an expression of frozen weariness. I could imagine the turmoil that had to be buried somewhere under that blank surface.

"I'm sorry, Glen," I said quietly. "I wish I could spare you all this, but I can't."

Joyce cut in. "What are you talking about, Gail?" It came out in a short of shrill squeak, very unlike her usual cool detachment.

I turned to face her, and she went on angrily. "Glen is very tired; he was just released from the hospital. He's not to be disturbed. Now I want all of you to leave right now, so he can get some rest."

I got the copper bar out of my pocket and held it out on the flat of my hand. "This mean anything to you, Joyce?"

It stopped her in midtirade. She opened her mouth and shut it, and her eyes were suddenly frightened.

"That's right," I said slowly. "I found it in your purse."

I held the bar out so the rest of the room could see it. Glen's eyes flicked to it quickly and then back to Joyce's face.

"What is it?" From Lisa.

I could see in Glen's look of sick recognition that he knew what it was. He just stared at Joyce, not saying a word.

"It's a solid copper bar, the same size as an electrical fuse," I told Lisa. "Electricians use them instead of fuses to connect something they don't want to short out under any circumstances, like a ground wire. They call them dummy fuses. I found this one in Joyce's purse when I searched her room this morning."

Nobody said a word. Glen was staring at Joyce, and Joyce was staring at me. Lisa's eyes were sharp, moving from one to another. Tim still stood near the French doors, his face smooth as a stone. You could have cut the tension in the room with a knife.

I looked right at Joyce. "I think that someone took all the spare fuses out of the fuse box and left this copper bar on the fuse shelf. Then this someone made a point of turning on the heater in the timer's shack in order to blow out the system. Glen goes in, flips the master switch to turn the power off, and walks to the fuse box to put in a fuse. He can't find a fuse, only this copper bar. I don't know if he knew what it was and decided to use it anyway, just to get the lights on, or whether in the dark he thought it was a fuse. Either way, he plugged it in. And someone had turned the power back on. When Glen plugged that solid copper bar into the system with the power on, it was certain to electrocute him. And it did."

Everyone was staring at me now. "I suspected it was you, Joyce. You had the opportunity; you were in and around the timer's shack; it would have been easy for you to do. But you got too clever. If you'd have left everything alone, it would have passed as an accident, probably. A suspicious one, maybe, but possible—just. But you were worried. So you turned the power back off again and you retrieved the dummy fuse. That was stupid. Because it was obvious that the accident simply could not have happened with the main switch off. It took me a while, but eventually I figured out how it could have happened. I searched your room because I thought you might have used something like this." I flipped the copper bar in my hand.

Joyce looked like a cornered coyote. She'd taken a couple of steps backward until she was up against the door to the room, and the look in her eyes was desperate. Desperate and something else. Savagely angry. She appeared torn between fight and flight.

I had already decided that the frilly white blouse and tight black jeans she was wearing could not possibly conceal a gun. She carried no purse; she stood near no drawers. I pressed her.

"Running won't help, Joyce. The cops will catch up in the end. Why'd you do it?" I asked softly.

The flat blue eyes looked right at me. Anger struggled with fear and anger won. "Because I hate the son of a bitch." Her face seemed to contort, the rage that had been penned up so long rushing out in a tide of ugly, corrosive venom. "Yeah, I hated him," she spit out. "The great Glen Bennett." Her eyes flashed at the quiet figure on the bed. "With his ranch and his family and his horses. I wasn't important to him at all. I was just a convenience, a token wife. He didn't give a damn about me." She stared at Glen as if she could make him disappear with the pure force of her hatred.

Lisa was watching Joyce with an expression of horror on her face. I felt pretty horrified myself. It was hard to reconcile the calm, cold exterior I was used to with the raging Joyce in front of me. This woman had been terribly angry for a long time and couldn't or wouldn't express it. Unbidden, a vignette from my youth flashed into my mind—Joyce, in one of her rare good moods, playing a cute, kittenish little girl to Glen's strong, silent man routine. Joyce, I thought, had never been able to deal with the frustration she felt at being forced into that role.

She was expressing a lot more than frustration now. "I did things just to make his life miserable. I left the gates open; I even tried to poison his stupid horses. I left the tractor in gear. I dug a hole in the arena; I thought maybe it would kill him."

I shot a glance at Glen. His eyes were closed and he leaned back on the pillows. He hadn't said a word since I'd walked into the room.

I cut in on Joyce. "We're talking about attempted murder, Joyce. You'll go to jail."

"I didn't murder him." Her voice rose. "Look at him; he's still alive."

"What did you give Smoke?" I asked her.

"Give Smoke?" For a second she looked confused; I watched her eyes drop and rise again and saw fear creep back in.

"Who gave you the dummy fuse and told you how to use it?" I asked.

"No one. It was my idea."

"And was it your idea to shoot at me this afternoon?"

"I never shot at you." Joyce's eyes jumped to my face.

"Well, someone did. I can prove it," I said firmly, not sure if I could or not. "And I *will* press charges."

"I didn't do it."

"So, who did?"

"I don't know."

"Yes, you do. You told someone that I found the dummy fuse; you told them where I was. And that someone shot at me with a deer rifle this afternoon. Who was it?"

Joyce shook her head. "I don't know."

"Yes, you do, Joyce. The same person who cut the colt's throat and gave Smoke a shot. And if you don't want to go to jail, you'll tell me who that person is."

She stared at me and licked her lips. I didn't take my eyes off her. I didn't know anymore what Lisa was doing, how Glen or Tim was reacting. I just watched Joyce.

"Tell me who it is," I prompted.

"I can't," she said softly.

"You have to. I'll turn you in to the police right now if you don't tell me." I glanced meaningfully at the phone by the bed. "Now, Joyce."

There was a second of silence while Joyce's eyes darted around the room frantically. I could imagine her brain doubling back on itself, trying to see a way out. I took a step toward the phone.

"All right. I'll tell you. I'll tell you who it is." She'd made up her mind. Her eyes whipped sharply across the room, and she pointed right at Tim. "He did."

Even as the words left her mouth there was a crashing boom. Red flowered on the white lacy front of Joyce's blouse, like a corsage.

Then she was falling and shards of glass were falling from the windows and Lisa ran to Joyce where she lay on the carpet. The blood was pumping out of the hole in her chest, and she made one choked moan. Lisa was trying to stanch the flow of blood with the hem of the bedspread.

"Call nine-one-one," I said to Glen. "Get help."

I saw him reach for the phone, and then I was out through the French doors, running across the dark lawn and seeing Tim running in front of me.

TWENTY-FIVE

The moon was up and Tim was a sharply defined black shape moving fast across the silver gray of the grass. I chased after him, my heart pounding with fear and adrenaline. I lost sight of him in the trees, but I could hear him, crashing and stumbling and swearing.

I charged in his wake, following the sounds of breaking branches. The darkness under the trees seemed absolute. I stumbled and nearly fell and bounced off an oak tree and kept running.

Then we were out on the road and I could see Tim, running flat-out down the hill, and ahead of him was another shape— a man, running, and Tim was gaining on him.

My heart was crashing in my chest. I saw the running man stop and take up a shooting stance. He had a rifle in his hands, and he was pointing it at Tim.

"Down, Tim!" I screamed. "Down!"

The shot cracked; Tim dove; the man whirled and ran again. I didn't think, just ran after him as hard as I could run. I had to catch him.

The dark figure ahead of me was down the hill, headed toward the roping area and the road, but I was gaining on him. He stopped and I heard another crack as I flung myself sideways. My gut lurched with fear, but there was no impact, no pain, and I plowed on, chasing him, drawing closer.

This was the shadowy figure who had pushed Joyce to murder Glen, tried to kill me, and shot Joyce just now. I wanted him, wanted to see his face, wanted his destruction.

He was at the arena fence, and he paused. He moved forward again, climbing over the fence, and I could see the shape of his head and his body clearly in the moonlight and knew for certain who I was chasing.

I slowed down. I could hear Tim behind me with a rush of running footfalls, and before I could say a word, he was past me and vaulting the fence. I looked ahead and saw that the dark figure we were chasing had stopped and was pointing the gun right at Tim.

I yelled frantically, "Stop!"

Everything seemed to freeze. The man with the rifle stood perfectly still, pointing the gun at Tim, who had lurched to a stop in midstride, as though he were playing Red Light—Green Light.

There was a long, strange moment of silence. I was aware of the three-quarter moon, high and hard and white in the sky behind me, shining down into *his* face. I could see some movement in the pens behind the chute, off to our right. Cattle, I thought. Everything around me was normal and familiar, except the gun that gleamed dully in the moonlight. I leaned on the rails of the fence, looking right along the barrel.

My heart was pounding hard from fear and exertion, but I tried to keep all that out of my voice when I spoke. I looked right at him, our unknown killer, and knew him all right. "Well, Charles," I said slowly.

He stared back at me. The moonlight seemed almost as bright on his face as daylight, but his eyes were just dark sockets—unreadable. I couldn't tell what he was thinking. His voice came as a shock. The arrogant confidence seemed undiminished, though he sounded out of breath. "Too bad for you, you nosy little bitch." He took a breath. "You made a mistake, coming after me."

He looked down the barrel of the rifle as he spoke, sighting carefully, pointing it not at me, but at Tim. "Climb over the fence, bitch," he said heavily. "Real slow. And come stand here by this asshole."

"It won't work, Charles," I said sharply. "Too many people know."

"Too bad." He still stared down the gun at Tim. "You two are gonna die. You first, you bastard Bennett. But you, you lousy little vet, are gonna get it, too. I should have made sure you were dead this afternoon. Now, climb over that fence, or I'll shoot little Bennett right in front of you."

I started climbing. I could hear Tim's voice, sounding bizarrely normal, his usual relaxed drawl. "Just couldn't handle it, could you, Charles? You're so damn jealous of Dad you had to kill him to get even."

Charles kept the gun trained on Tim. "Kill him because he's a bastard. He deserves it."

I was over the fence now. Tim's quiet voice went on. "Kill him because he's a better man and your wife knows it."

I saw the infinitesimal jerk of the gun as it went off. The shot shattered the night, and I dove straight at Charles.

I hit him right at the knees, even as another dark shape came out of the night from my right and hit both of us. I felt a crashing punch in my right shoulder; then Charles went down and the gun went off again. Someone was on top of Charles and was smashing his fist into Charles's belly. Whump. Charles groaned.

Twisting myself away, I spotted the metallic gleam of the gun and grabbed it out of a slack hand. Charles writhed, and I heard another whump. There was a loud moan, and then a voice I recognized. "Don't move," it said heavily to Charles.

215

I got to my feet, holding the rifle gingerly. "Thanks, Al," I said.

Al Borba crouched over Charles in the moonlight, gripping Charles's shirt with one hand, his heavy frame gorillalike in its stance, his arm cocked back to deal another blow. There was no need. Charles was gasping in painful wheezes, like a punctured balloon.

I looked for Tim. He sat on the ground, holding his right shoulder with his left hand; I could see the dark stain in the moonlight.

"He hit you; you're bleeding." I squatted next to Tim.

He flexed his right arm slowly. "Not serious. Just winged me." I could hear a trace of a drawl. "It all works."

Tim got up slowly and we both looked at Charles and Al, still frozen in their tableau. "I've got his gun, Al. You can let go of him." When Al took a step toward Tim and me, I trained the rifle on Charles's prone form.

"Where were you?" I asked Al.

"In the pen with the cattle," he said. "I saw that horse running around the barn about half an hour ago, so I went over and unsaddled him and put him away and turned off the lights. Then I went out here to check on these weaned calves; a couple of them didn't look so good this morning. That's when I heard the shots and saw you running down the hill. I turned off my flashlight and waited. After a while I figured out what was going on."

"Well, thanks," I said.

Al was silent.

We all stared down at Charles. He was still gasping where he lay on the ground, and both arms were wrapped around his stomach.

"So it was this asshole all the time," Tim said.

"I don't know about all the time. Joyce set up most of the little accidents that Lisa noticed. But he's the one who pushed Joyce toward murder. And he just shot her."

"Yeah." Tim looked at me. "I don't know why she pointed at me, Gail. I mean, we've never liked each other, and ever since Dad got electrocuted I've been watching her like a hawk, 'cause I wondered, but I sure never had anything to do with this bullshit."

"I know," I told him. "Joyce was desperate to put the blame on somebody, anybody that wasn't Charles. Charles was her lover."

We both looked down at the figure on the ground. "I knew Joyce had some kind of an ally; I didn't believe she was capable of some of the accidents. And I think she was protecting him because of their 'relationship.' And I guess he was waiting out there in the dark to kill Glen. He came after me this afternoon and shot at me and thought he killed me. I think he was starting to believe he could get away with anything."

Charles was still gasping and moaning a little. I kept the gun pointed at him; he seemed to be getting his air back. As we watched, he pushed himself up into a sitting position.

"Don't move," I said.

He glanced up at me and the gun and the two men beside me and didn't seem inclined to try. Just sat there, with his head down, breathing hard. He was a bully, I thought, used to victims who couldn't or wouldn't fight back. A little physical damage to his own person was more than he could stand.

"Listen." Tim pointed with his good hand toward the road.

We could all hear the sirens. Glen had gotten help.

"Go get some of them to come here," I asked Al. "Tim needs someone to look at that shoulder, and we need people to take him away." I pointed with the rifle at Charles.

Al stumped off, going toward the road. Charles sat with his head bowed, the picture of defeat. I felt no sorrow or sympathy for him; it was hard for me to see him as human. I had tracked him down with a tenacity I hadn't known I possessed, and now that I had defeated him, I felt not satisfaction, but a deep grief for all that he had destroyed. Life would never be the same.

"You killed Joyce," I said out loud.

"I didn't give a damn about Joyce." The old arrogance was a _int echo in his voice. "Joyce was my mistress, but she didn't _ean one thing to me. I used her to get at Glen."

"Why'd you shoot her?" I asked him.

"She gave me away. I stood right outside those windows. I _rd her. She said I did it."

"She didn't give you away, Charles," I told him. "She covered _ou right until the very end. Until you killed her."

He didn't say anything for a minute. When he spoke it was as if to himself. "I didn't give a damn about her. But I hated that bastard. He took Pat away from me. Everyone knew. I did it for Pat." The force with which he said that brought on a fit of coughing. When he finished, he looked straight at me. "I should have made sure you were dead."

I nodded slowly. "Yeah. I guess you should have."

TWENTY-SIX

Three days later I sat in the bar at Casa del Mar, sipping a margarita and staring out the window at a stream of black shorebirds—shearlings—flying endlessly (or so it seemed) to the south.

Lonny sat beside me, looking over the bay, his shoulder just touching mine. All around us groups of suntanned golfers and tennis players chattered and drank, munching tortilla chips with abandon. Casa del Mar, the dining room of the old Rio del Mar Hotel, with its ancient adobe walls and dramatic site on a cliff overlooking Monterey Bay, was very popular with the local country club set.

Lonny and I stood out a bit, I thought with amusement. In our jeans and work shirts and boots, neither of us entirely free from dirt and both slightly speckled with flecks of the alfalfa hay we'd been moving, we looked a good deal more rumpled and untidy than the rest of the crowd.

"Lisa called me today," I said, still staring at the flying stream of shearlings.

"What did she say?" Lonny asked. "How's Glen?"

"Glen's OK. She says he won't talk about Joyce or Charles or any of that, and he's still weak, so she isn't pressing him. The one person he'll talk to is Al Borba, she says. They talk about the ranch just like nothing ever happened, and even though he's on crutches, Glen goes out every morning to talk to Al about the day's chores. Lisa thinks he'll be OK."

"That's good."

"She says Al and Janey are both being really helpful. She's surprised. Maybe they just want to hang onto a deal where they don't have to pay rent. Janey brings cookies or a cake up almost every day, and Lisa thinks that Al is really making a point of letting Glen lean on him."

"How's Tim?"

"He's fine. It wasn't a serious wound. His shoulder's taped up, but Lisa says he'll be one hundred percent in a couple of weeks. She's been talking to him a lot, she told me. He wants to talk, I guess. He told her he'd gotten so resentful of Glen that he felt he almost hated him. It took Glen getting electrocuted and nearly dying to wake Tim up. Suddenly he knew he loved his dad. At that point, everything Lisa had been saying got through to him and he was really afraid for Glen. That's why he wouldn't leave his side.

"I guess he suspected right away it was Joyce; he'd been living in the same house with the two of them for years, after all. He was afraid if he left Glen even for a minute, Joyce would finish the job. He might have been right."

"Joyce's funeral is tomorrow," Lonny said quietly.

"That's right. Will you go with me?"

"If you want." Lonny sighed. "How's Lisa doing?"

"Good. Or so she says. She told me her ex, Sonny, showed up the other night, acting apologetic and offering sympathy. Told her he wanted to get back together. Lisa said she just listened and then let him know she wasn't interested; he left with his tail between his legs, in her words. She told me she finally feels in charge of her life again. She's not afraid of Sonny anymore."

"That's great." Lonny was quiet a moment. "How are you feeling about all this?" he asked me.

"I don't know. In a sense, I feel I failed. Lisa asked me to help her, and even though I tried, Joyce is still dead."

"But Glen's alive."

"Yes. Glen's alive."

"And Charles is in jail."

"Uh huh." We were both silent. After a minute, I said, "I saw Pat down at the sheriff's office when I gave them my statement."

"How did she seem?"

"Worn down, but still Pat. She was friendly. I asked her how she was doing, and she said she was surviving. Then she told me that even though this terrible thing had happened, in a way it had helped her. She realized what a farce her life with Charles had been. She said she went to see him in jail and he seemed like a stranger. She couldn't believe she hadn't left him years ago."

More quiet. I thought that becoming strangers looked like one of the occupational hazards of being married. In Pat's case, the results had been pretty extreme. And in Glen's.

"So, how do you like your new horse?" I asked Lonny, changing the subject.

Instantly his wide grin creased his face. "Just fine," he said happily. "I'm glad you talked me into that. I roped half a dozen practice steers on him this morning, and we're getting along great."

I smiled back at him. To my satisfaction, he had made a deal to buy Chester from Glen. "That horse is a good one," I'd told him.

Lonny opened his mouth to say something and then shut it suddenly. All the light seemed to die out of his eyes. I turned my head to follow his gaze, which had fixed on the entrance to the bar.

A woman in a white dress walked through the archway. She had smooth, shiny brown hair, and she was followed by a tall man in a gray suit. My eyes swung back to her, and my heart jumped. It was Sara.

The two of them came walking along the bar in our direction. When they were opposite our table, Lonny cleared his throat and stood up. "Hello, Sara," he said.

Sara glanced at us, at first casually, then with sudden intensity. Her chin lifted and she turned her face a fraction, enough that her eyes missed mine and rested directly on Lonny.

"Hello," she said.

There was a moment of awkward silence. Then the tall man behind Sara stepped forward and held out his hand. "I'm Alan Todd," he said. He looked as relaxed as Sara was tense.

Lonny shook the man's hand. "Lonny Peterson. This is Gail McCarthy," he replied, gesturing at me.

I smiled.

Sara's back was straight and stiff. "Lonny's my ex-husband," she said briefly. Managing a civil smile at the two of us, she turned to her companion. "Shall we check our reservations?"

"All right. Nice to meet you." Alan Todd smiled cordially in our direction, and the two of them departed.

"Whew." Lonny looked at me.

I smiled. "I don't think she was very glad to see you."

"No."

"She did call you her ex, though."

"I noticed. And it looks like she might have a new boyfriend."

"Yeah, it does. How do you feel about that?"

"Happy for her."

I nodded. I was being surprised by how much it wasn't bothering me to see Sara. I'd been jealous of her for years, in the last six months almost pathologically so, and now, it seemed, she made no difference at all.

"You don't want to be back with her?" I asked Lonny.

"No," he said. "I've decided to get the divorce."

"No matter what?"

"No matter what. It's something I need to do for me."

"What made you come to that decision?"

Lonny looked out the window, where dusk was darkening the sky above the tranquil waters of the bay. "She isn't a part of my life," he said at last. "I need to recognize that."

I took a long swallow of margarita. We both ate a few chips. The silence was the silence of two people thinking hard. Lonny broke it. "How did you know it was Joyce who set up those accidents?"

I thought a minute. "I didn't know. But it seemed obvious to me that the person who arranged the bulk of the accidents had to live on the ranch. It would have been possible for an outsider to have set up one or two little disasters. But not a whole string. It would have been too risky. So, from almost the beginning, I thought the stalker had to be Tim or Joyce or Al or Janey. For a long time I suspected Tim. It was only after Glen got electrocuted that I really thought about Joyce. She was in the right place at the right time, and you know what they say about a spouse being the number-one suspect. So I followed my hunch.

"What I think now is that Joyce's affair with Charles was the catalyst that unleashed all the resentment she felt toward Glen. She started acting that resentment out by setting up accidents to make his life miserable, and, eventually, she told Charles what she was doing.

"Charles hated Glen because he thought Glen was having an affair with Pat. His affair with Joyce was mostly in the nature of revenge on Glen. When Joyce told him about her 'accidents,' he got the idea he could really avenge himself.

"I think he was the one who came up with the more serious accidents. I think he gave Joyce the shot to give Smoke, and I think he was the one who killed the colt. I'm sure he thought up the 'accident' with the dummy fuse and told Joyce what to do. He meant for Glen to die. But that's where Joyce made a mistake. She got scared. If she'd left the dummy fuse in place and the power switched on, I might have believed it was an accident. It would have been hard to prove that it wasn't. But she tried to be too careful, now that they were actually trying to murder Glen. She hid the fuse in her purse and tuned the power off."

I took a long swallow of margarita.

"How could she do that?" Lonny sounded genuinely uncomprehending.

"Being married can do some funny things to people. You know that."

As far as inadequate conclusions went, that one probably took the cake. There just wasn't much else to say. The way people felt when they got close to each other and then came apart—those were the strongest emotions in the world, maybe.

"But what in the world would Glen have done that caused her to hate him enough to try to kill him?"

I sighed. "I don't know, of course. But pride was a big part of what Glen was. Pride in himself, in what he stood for. I don't think he really had much else. His relationship with Joyce was empty; Glen wasn't himself; he was performing a role, all based on his pride. I think Joyce grew to hate him for that. I know Tim resented him deeply."

"So now what?"

"I don't know." It was repetitive but true. "Glen probably feels like a complete failure. His pride in that image of himself that he held up for so long is all torn down. That pride was his strength. I've come to understand it probably isn't a good kind of strength, but I admired Glen for it for years."

Lonny nodded.

"Maybe Glen will get more in touch with who he really is through all this. I don't know. Maybe, in the end, he'll be a happier person."

Outside, I could see wisps of fog starting to drift in over the bay. Reflexively, I shivered, and Lonny put his arm around me. "Will you stay at my house tonight?" he said quietly. "I want to hold you."

I looked at him. His steady green eyes met mine without a flicker.

"Yes," I said. "I will." I took his hand and held it. "Thank you," I told him.

"For what?" He sounded genuinely puzzled.

"For being you."

TWENTY-SEVEN

Three months later, Lonny and I sat on the grassy south-facing slope in front of my new house in Corralitos while I explained my plans for the two-and-a-half-acre property. Every few minutes this explanation was interrupted as we were attacked by a small, furry ball of energy—my eight-week-old puppy, Roey.

Everything seemed to have happened with amazing speed. My old house sold quickly; miraculously, during the escrow period I found this property, which fitted all my needs and was within my budget. And moving into my new place coincided with the date when Lisa's puppies were ready to leave their mother.

True to her word, Lisa had given me the pick of the litter; I'd chosen a red female pup, neither the largest nor the smallest of the seven siblings, but one who seemed to have a sweet disposition and a bright eye. At eight weeks, she looked like a fluffy baby bear cub, in miniature. I'd named her Roey in honor of her parents, and she was already doing a lot to fill the gap Blue had left.

At the moment, she was chewing on Lonny's boot, while he

made laughing efforts to repulse her. "I liked it better when you had an old dog," he told me.

"Things change," I said lightly.

The understatement of the century. Things had changed a hell of a lot, lately.

"I had dinner with Lisa last night," I said. "She says Glen seems to be pulling out of his depression. He's off his crutches and he's riding again. Al's helped a lot, according to Lisa. She can hardly believe how supportive he's been of Glen."

"What about Tim?"

"He left to go work for a horse trainer. I think he finally realized it was time for him to leave home and try life on his own."

"Good." Lonny's nod was emphatic.

"Lisa said Pat's been over a few times; she thinks that maybe Glen will start seeing Pat openly, eventually."

"When's Charles's trial?"

"Another month. Since they're holding him without bail, it's not too big of an issue. He won't get out of jail for a long time. There's plenty of evidence to convict him of second-degree murder, at least, if nothing else."

Lonny said nothing; I knew he, like me, was contemplating the pure unreality of the devastation Charles had wrought on the outwardly tranquil world of Lone Oak.

"Of course, it wasn't peaceful before, not really," I said out loud. "All that hatred and unhappiness was there, under the surface. It's just out in the open now."

"It's probably better this way." Lonny said it reluctantly; I wasn't sure he really meant it. Lonny had a strong interest in keeping things stable and serene.

"In a lot of ways I think it *is* better," I said. "But Joyce is dead. And so are three good horses."

"And Charles is in jail, probably for life," Lonny added.

"I'm sorry, but I can't feel much regret about that. I don't even think I'd feel regret if Charles were dead. I don't see one redeeming human quality in Charles."

228

We were both silent. I was thinking of that long afternoon in Glen's back pasture when Charles had stalked me with his rifle. If I had moved too soon, I wouldn't be here now. Uncontrollably, I shuddered a little.

Lonny put his arm around me. "So," he said, "are we going to get married?" His tone was friendly, casual, but I heard the underlying sincerity and hope. It made it harder to say what I knew I had to say.

"I don't want to get married," I said. "Not yet, anyway."

Lonny absorbed this, his face quiet. He plucked a stalk of wild oats and picked the seed heads off one by one. When the last grain was gone, he asked, "Do you still love me?"

"Yes," I said.

"What does that mean?"

I studied the familiar fifty-year-old countenance. Not handsome, no longer mysteriously unknown, but kind and intelligent.

"I think loving a person is a lot like loving a dog or a horse," I told him.

"So what does that mean?"

"It means," I said, "not quitting."

"So we go on loving each other?"

I took his hand and held it. "Yes," I said. "Always."